D1082650

SAINT PHILIP OF THE JOYOUS HEART

SAINT PHILIP OF THE JOYOUS HEART

Written by Francis X. Connolly

Illustrated by Lili Rethi

IGNATIUS PRESS SAN FRANCISCO

Originally published by Farrar, Straus & Cudahy, Inc.
A Vision Book
Published with ecclesiastical approval
Reprinted with permission of
Farrar, Straus & Giroux, Inc., New York

Cover design by Riz Boncan Marsella
Cover illustration by Christopher J. Pelicano

With ecclesiastical approval
Published by Ignatius Press, San Francisco, 1993

ISBN 978-0-89870-431-0
Library of Congress catalogue number 92-74761
Printed at Brilliant Printers Pvt. Ltd, Bangalore, India; D0884, November, 2016

CONTENTS

Author's Note 7
1. Pippo Buono—Good Little Phil 11
2. Long Live Florence! 20
3. Siege 36
4. Farewell to Florence 48
5. Philip Tries to Be a Merchant 59
6. A Pilgrimage to Gaeta 69
7. Philip Goes to Rome 80
8. The Globe of Fire 96
9. Philip Becomes a Priest 110
10. Tried by Fire 127
11. Philip Founds the Oratory 145
12. "Give Me My Love Quickly" 157

AUTHOR'S NOTE

The main purpose of this book is to acquaint younger readers with a great friend of Christ, another Christ, to use the consecrated words of Catholic Tradition. For some strange reason this extravagantly loving and lovable Saint Philip is not well known in English-speaking lands. He should be. Like Saint Francis of Assisi, he is one of the most childlike of God's servants and, characteristically, a lover of children. He was, too, a mighty force in the true reformation of the Church. In his *A Popular History of the Reformation,* Father Philip Hughes writes that the conversion of Rome "was the influence, radically, of a single man, the Florentine, Saint Philip Neri, an utterly unusual, unconventional character". His spirit, expressed in his own saying, "A joyous heart is more easily made perfect than one that is cast down", inspired his own generation. It is no less necessary today. Saint Philip of the Joyous Heart, pray for us.

The historical background for this book is drawn largely from standard biographies of Saint Philip Neri: *The Life of St. Philip* by Fathers Ricci and Bacci (1622), in the translation by Father Faber; *The Life of St. Philip* by Alfonso Capecelatro (2 volumes, 1882); *St. Philip Neri and the Roman Society of His Times* by Louis Ponelle and Louis Bordet, New York (1933); and *St. Philip Neri* by V. J. Matthews, London (1934). I have found other material in the lives of saints and popes who were Saint Philip's contemporaries, notably in Father James Brodrick's biographies of Saint Ignatius Loyola, Saint Francis Xavier, and his other writings on the founding fathers of the Society of Jesus. Ludwig von Pastor's *The History of the Popes* and Father Philip Hughes' *History of the Church* provided additional material, as did special histories on Rome and Florence during the sixteenth century.

For the most part this story adheres to the biographical facts. With the exception of the two monks who appear in chapter 10, and one or two incidental characters, the names are of actual persons. Philip's prayers and his prayerful thoughts are either direct quotations or slight adaptations of the prayers or sayings recorded in the standard lives.

Saint Philip's early life, developed in chapters 1–6, is known in outline but not in detail. I have adhered to the outline and supplied some probable, and some merely possible, details. The incident of the donkey in chapter 1 did take place at the farm; the incidental details are my own. Saint Philip did attend Ser Vincente's school (chapter 2), but that he actually participated in the other events described in chapters 2–3 is reasonably surmised.

Author's Note

There is no authentic account of the journey to San Germano or the pilgrimage to Gaeta (chapters 5–6) but Tradition is strong that he was undergoing the spiritual testing described in the pages relating these events. In chapter 7 the main events did occur, but not necessarily in the order they are presented, since the chronology here is foreshortened. The verses ascribed to Saint Philip are not his, but (hopefully) modern equivalents of the kind of joke and the kind of simple pious hymn he used for the entertainment and instruction of young and old alike. Saint Philip probably did meet Saint Francis Xavier—Tradition has it in the very hospital named in chapter 8—but the particular circumstance in this story is only a likely supposition. On the other hand, the accounts of Buonsignore Cacciaguerra, Teccosi, and the two monks—seemingly too dramatic to be true—are as close to the literal facts as the limitations of this book allow. The materials in chapters 11 and 12 are abridgments of the immense activity of the last two decades of Philip's life.

I

PIPPO BUONO—GOOD LITTLE PHIL

ONE DAY in the early summer of 1521, Ser Francesco di Filippo di Neri complained to his wife Maria, "Bah! There is no sense in my going to work today. There are no contracts for notaries to witness anyhow. In all of Florence—indeed, in all of Italy—they talk of nothing but war and famine."

Maria knew one sure way to cure her husband's gloom. They would have a day in the country with the children. She knew how much Francesco loved his children. Lisabetta, a dark-haired little girl with the voice of a lark, would tease him with smiles.

Caterina, grave, modest, olive-skinned, would soothe him with her "Yes, Papa", and her swift, smooth obedience to his wishes.

But most of all he would delight in being with his only son, Filippo, his Pippo Buono, his good little Phil. Philip was now six years old. Even among the Florentines he was small for his age. He hopped around like a sparrow and talked like a streak all day long. He radiated joy and trust. Yes, Philip would bring joy to Francesco's heart. Maria felt a tug at her own heart, for she, too, loved her stepson with a special intensity she could not account for.

"Francesco," she said, "do not go to the Hall of Notaries. It is too beautiful a day. Let us go instead to the farm. I need some fresh eggs and cheese. It is time, too, that you talked with Giacomo about the wine for the new year."

Ser Francesco's face suddenly lost its crease of care. He always loved to visit the old family farm at Castelfranco just outside the city. In his mind's eye he could see himself lying under the pine tree on the hill overlooking Florence. He would drink a cup of wine with his tenant, Giacomo, and watch the children play.

"Well," he said, "since you need eggs and cheese I suppose we should go."

"Come, children", Maria said before he could change his mind. "Caterina, bring a basket for the eggs and cheese. Lisabetta, fetch your father's walking boots. Philip, wear your straw hat; it will be hot in the sun."

Soon the Neri family was on the road to Castelfranco, Philip and Lisabetta skipping on ahead chattering, and sedate Caterina walking primly just in front of her parents. Ser Francesco and Maria drank in the sweet, flower-scented air.

Suddenly Ser Francesco burst out laughing. "Ho, ho, ho! Just look at Philip."

Little Phil was matching strides with Lisabetta, his rough straw hat flopping over his ears. To keep up with his sister he was jumping like a grasshopper.

"Run on ahead, child," her step-mother said to Caterina as they neared the farm, "and tell Giacomo we are coming. He does not like to be surprised."

A few minutes later Giacomo, his eyes bright, came to meet them. He bowed to Francesco and kissed Maria's hand as his leathery face cracked into a wide smile.

"How fortunate that you have come today! Look what I have for you."

He pointed to a mound of vegetables—yellow squash; round, lemon-colored melons; green cabbages; carrots rusty red with the earth clinging to them; purple grapes; and small, wrinkled green apples.

"We will pack them on the donkey, no? Then you can have an easy walk home."

Giacomo led the grown-ups into the shade alongside the stone house. They sat down on the bench facing the farmyard.

"Now, children," Maria said, "enjoy yourselves. Run about and play for a while."

To Philip everything on the farm seemed alive. He ran first to the big, knobby tree whose branches hung over the well. Then he crossed the yard to the barn, said hello a little timidly to Bobo, the great white ox, and patted the thick folds on his neck. He visited Eugenia, the old sow, squishing the mud in her pen, and threw her a few tattered cabbage leaves. The gray cat had four new kittens, so Philip made friends with them. He made friends all over again with Beppo, the fat, shaggy dog.

Tiring of this, he joined his sisters who were drawing circles in the dust for a game of hippity-hop. Philip played with them until his mother called out: "Children, we are going inside with Giacomo. Don't play too hard in the sun."

The little girls both said, "Yes, Mama", and at once went dutifully to a spot where the branches of a stunted oak shaded the slate-hooded well. Philip went to see the donkey, already loaded with baskets of food and skins of wine for the journey home.

"I am talking to my friend", Philip said to his sisters. "Look, he knows me." The donkey's nose rested on Philip's shoulder. "He recognizes me as a brother." They laughed, and Caterina called out, "Fetch me his pail. I will draw a fresh drink of water for him."

Ser Francesco and Maria went into the farmhouse. The earthen floor was damp and cool, the darkness a relief from the sun's glare. Scarcely had they sat down at the long oak table when they heard the sound of scraping, a great thud, and the girls' shrieking, mingled with the braying of the donkey.

Ser Francesco ran to the door. "Jesu, Maria", he gasped.

The donkey had fallen backwards down the outer stairs to the cellar. He saw the four small hoofs pawing the air, like the claws of an upended turtle. Smashed squash, burst melons, crushed grapes, shattered cabbages were strewn on the cellar stairs.

"Papa, Papa, Papa!" Caterina pulled at his arm frantically. "The donkey fell on Philip. . . ."

"He was jumping on the donkey's back", little Lisabetta added, tears running down her cheeks. "He's been bashed in like a melon."

"Oh, oh, oh!" Maria's voice was added to the hubbub. Giacomo ran from the barn. Suddenly the dog barked, and the chickens began to cluck excitedly. For one terrible moment Ser Francesco stood still, paralyzed with fear. He was . . . Philip was . . . dead—surely. Otherwise why did he not cry? Or was that his voice amid thc excited din made by the girls, his wife, the dogs, the chickens, and the still up-ended donkey?

Then, breaking the ice of fear, Ser Francesco ran down the cellar steps. Giacomo tumbled after him. Together they heaved the little donkey to his feet.

Ser Francesco bent over Philip. The little boy lay crumpled against the wooden cellar door. How white he looked in the dark well of the stairs! Ser Francesco knelt down, his hands trembling as he felt first Philip's neck, then his arms, his back, his legs. Philip gave a little moan. His eyelids fluttered as they did when he woke up after a long sleep.

"Philip, Philip!" Ser Francesco rubbed his son's hands gently. He hardly heard Giacomo lead the poor donkey up the steps. Nor did he notice that Maria, having brought the girls inside the house, was now at his side with a pail of water and white linen rags.

Absent-mindedly he held Philip on his lap while Maria swabbed the blue lump on Philip's forehead and washed clean the cut under his chin with the cool well water.

"There are no bones broken, Maria", he said hopefully.

"God grant his head and his insides are not hurt", she said, her gentle hands still bathing the boy's forehead. "He was jumping on the donkey's back and sliding off backwards. He lost his balance. When he fell, he reached for the poor beast's tail and pulled it on top of him, Caterina said. She was watching."

Philip opened dazed eyes, and a feeble little smile tugged at the corner of his mouth.

"Papa, Mama", he cried.

"Don't try to talk, Pippo", Maria said. And then, just like a mother, she asked quickly, "Do you feel a pain in your head? Or in your stomach?"

"I feel Papa trembling", Philip said. "Papa, you, too, have a donkey in your lap. Donkey Pippo."

Philip winced a little as he tried to bray like a donkey.

Francesco, relieved to see his son like his old self, laughed.

"It was no joke five minutes ago, Pippo. I . . . I . . . thought you were dead. My beard stood up in terror. I could feel it. There now, can you sit up? Easy, now."

He still held Philip on his lap. "Your head swims, doesn't it? Well, that will pass. Now promise me—never slide off the rear end of a donkey."

Maria discovered a cut on the back of Philip's head. "Bend your head, Pippo." She sloshed water over the cut.

Shakily Philip got to his feet. "I am all right. See? Not a bone broken, thanks be to God."

Philip was all right, but the donkey was limping

badly. Giacomo examined the beast carefully and then looked at Philip. An expression of awe crept over his strong, bronze face. He crossed himself.

"Messer Francesco", he said. "It is a miracle. The boy isn't hurt at all. But look, the donkey limps."

Francesco and Maria both felt the chill that comes from sudden wonder. A miracle! Yes, it was, Ser Francesco thought. Perhaps God wanted Philip to be one of his chosen few. Maria was thinking the same thing. Philip, her little son, looked like an angel—like the angel in the Giotto picture at the Santa Croce church. Over and over again she thanked the Virgin for sparing her son.

They did not go home until late in the afternoon. Then they walked very slowly, resting often lest Philip be overtired.

"You know, Maria," Ser Francesco said, "I am convinced that we *did* see a miracle happen. Do you think it means that our little Phil will become a priest?"

Maria lowered her voice so the children ahead of them could not hear her. "He is very good, Francesco, and he seems always to be drawn to the churches. Every day he is in and out of San Marco, San Giorgio, the Santa Croce. Oh, Francesco, even though he is our child and we can think no ill of him, I know there is something very special about him. Everyone calls him Pippo Buono."

Maria's words made Francesco happy, but worried too. What did one do with a saint in one's family? Certainly he must make sure that Philip went to a good school—to Ser Clemente's, if possible—where he would learn Latin and prepare for the university—or for the priesthood.

2

LONG LIVE FLORENCE!

OCTOBER 12, 1529, started as usual for Philip Neri. Maria came into his room and touched his shoulder. He bounced up. Then he knelt down and said an *Ave* with his mother.

Philip dressed quickly. Out of the house he ran and up the hill to the Church of San Giorgio, just as the sexton opened the door. He helped the old man pull the bell rope and scatter the sweet sounds over the valley of the Arno.

After Mass he ran down the cottage-crusted hill to his own house. There the morning sun was just slanting over the flower-covered garden wall, just fringing the red tiles on the sloping roof.

His mother had baked hard seed rolls and had warmed fresh milk for his breakfast. She stood over him while he ate.

"Yesterday you had nothing at all", she said reprovingly. "Today you must eat."

Philip was never hungry. When he had eaten as much as he could, he kissed his mother, gathered up his books, and started off to Ser Clemente's school.

From the suburb of San Giorgio, where the Neri house nestled in its hillside garden, Philip could look across the River Arno to the city of Florence itself. What a glittering sight it was that golden October morning in 1529! The four beautiful bridges seemed to be floating on their graceful arches over the tinted river. Beyond them the palace of the Signoria, where city business was conducted, the churches of San Marco, Santa Croce, San Michele, San Leonardo—and a dozen others—thrust their beautiful towers, domes, and spires into the azure sky.

Breathing in the pride and splendor of his city, Philip thanked God for letting him be a Florentine. He descended the hill and mingled with the throng on the *Ponte Vecchio* (the old bridge). Then Philip began to feel the true life of the city, its swift, human pulse. How quickly Florentines moved! Clerks and craftsmen, priests, nobles, tradesmen, porters were swarming into the city like bees humming to their hives. Today there was an almost feverish quickness about the throng.

In the main square a column of the militia was drawn up. A member of the government—the Great Council—stood beside a Dominican priest. Philip listened for a while as the councilman exhorted the soldiers.

"Florence is strong as well as beautiful. She will never give in to the emperor, Charles V, who wishes to destroy the republic and to restore the Medici as rulers of Florence. If there is a war, we will fight again—and conquer—under the banner of Christ. Those who are too young to fight will take the places of those who fight for them."

The great bells of San Marco clanged the hour, and flocks of pigeons swirled from their roosts in the towers and roofs, streaking the square with their scudding shadows. Eight o'clock! Ser Clemente would be angry with him if he were late.

He rushed up the Via Giulia, a mere slit between tall, ancient buildings, bumping into a fish peddler with a basket of pungent salt herring on his back.

"A thousand pardons", he panted.

He just made it in time. Nine of Ser Clemente's scholars were already at their benches, books opened, tablets in hand, ready for the lesson in

Latin. Philip scrambled to his seat as the master entered the room.

Messer Clemente was another reason why Philip loved Florence. Clemente was gentle and strong. His voice was musical, his gestures graceful but virile. He was learned in the ancient languages, in poetry and history. Yet he was full of good jokes, and he seemed to know, as if by instinct, when to say, "Let us put away our tablets and sing. What shall it be?"

What a joy it was to sing! There was nothing Philip loved more than the *laudi,* or hymns of praise, that the Florentines sang during their religious processions. Songs like the *laudi* made him think he was flying up to heaven.

Today, however, Messer Clemente seemed very grave. There were deep purple rings under his eyes, and his high forehead wore a frown of anxiety. There were no jokes during the morning lessons and, instead of reading Cacsar's *Gallic Wars,* they read a life of Saint Sebastian, the Roman soldier who died a martyr's death.

During the recess Philip went up to his silent master. "Messer Clemente," he said, "a penny for your thoughts."

"You little rascal." Ser Clemente playfully tweaked Philip's nose. "My thoughts *are* serious, Pippo. I can tell you this. The republic is in danger. Last night there was a meeting of the Great Council.

The council has called upon all the people to fast for twenty-four hours. Tomorrow there will be a great public reception of Holy Communion and a procession of all the people to beg God's help against our enemies."

Philip's heart skipped a beat. Young though he was, he still knew what war meant. Only last April the enemy had been outside the city walls. His mother had not forced him to eat then, for there had been nothing to eat.

Ser Clemente's hand was on his shoulder. "Don't lose your happy disposition, Pippo. God will preserve us as he has done in the past."

Then, with a sigh, Ser Clemente added, "I must join the militia. After today's lessons you will all be free from school for a while. But, Philip, you must keep up with your studies by yourself. I know in my heart that you will be a scholar. God willing, you may even enter the university next year. You are ready for it, Pippo. You will bring honor to my school."

Early in the afternoon Ser Clemente said farewell to his scholars. He told them all to go home immediately. Philip lingered awhile after the others left, reluctant to part with Messer Clemente. By the time he left the school, the Via Giulia had turned into a roaring river of excited men and women.

Everyone was rushing toward the square of San Marco. Cries of, "Long live Florence! Long live

General Nicolo Capponi! Long live the republic! Long live liberty!" resounded in the canyonlike street. Philip felt himself swept along in a frenzied tide of angry, fearful, shouting men. Adding to the din were the bells from a hundred churches clanging the call to assembly.

Philip pushed, and squirmed, and burrowed his way through the thronged streets toward the old bridge that led to San Giorgio. At the bridgehead an impatient herd of people milled and shuffled, moving forward by inches. Excitement, even terror, strained through men's faces. Women with small children screamed, "Let me through! Let me through!" But those ahead could not move because of the wall of people ahead of them. Still the bells clanged as if urging people on, on, on.

Philip was almost crushed between a burly peasant who reeked of garlic and sweat and a thin old man who seemed to be folded in his physician's robes.

"Ow," Philip cried out, "you're stepping on me."

The man from the country scowled. "Keep out of my way. It's every man for himself today."

Finally a mounted militiaman maneuvered his horse into the middle of the crowd. "Single file to the right, single file to the right", he bawled. "Carry all children or they'll be stamped to death."

The mob swirled around the militiaman like mill

water around a rock. Philip followed the peasant across the bridge. Once he was on the other side of the river the crowd thinned out. Save for the steadily booming bells, the suburb of San Giorgio was quiet.

When Philip entered the house his mother and sisters were packing the great iron-handled oak chest. Maria was sobbing. She ran to him and embraced him.

"Philip, Philip," she cried, "thank God you're safe. It's terrible, terrible. . . ."

He hated to see his mother cry. Her eyelids, drawn tight to keep back the tears, twitched and fluttered, her hands trembled, her voice quavered.

"Philip, we must leave our beautiful house. Your father sent word for us to go back to the city. He has found us a place inside the walls at the house of Luca di Raggiamonte, the apothecary. Your father is busy at the Signoria notarizing lists for the militia. Oh, what will become of us? What will become of us?"

Philip put his arms around his mother. He patted her wet cheeks and caressed her hands. "Don't cry, don't cry", he kept repeating. "Papa is wise. He knows what is best." Eventually his mother grew calm.

"Caterina," she said, "do not forget to put in the needles and thread. There will be a shortage, as there was last time. Be sure to pack Papa's parchments and quills. Lisabetta, help me in the kitchen. Wrap the sausages and cheese. You, Philip, like a good boy, bundle up all the books and the candles. Tie them well."

By dusk, they had finished packing. The evening star was in the east; the wind blew gently from the mountain. It was a night more suited for a quiet walk under the sky than for running away.

Philip grabbed one end of the chest, Caterina the other. As they lurched down the hill the handle cut into Philip's hands. Caterina stumbled and the chest slid forward, digging into his back. Philip staggered, almost fell, but Lisabetta, dropping her basket of food, rushed to steady him.

"Be careful, children; go slowly", Maria implored.

Down at the bridge they had to wait their turn to cross, for now all the countryside, alarmed by the bells, crowded toward the protection of the city's walls. In the glare of the pine torches Philip saw shadowy figures staggering under heaped baskets.

Within the city the nervous, swishing crowds in the marketplace blocked their passage. Torch lights and lanterns flared and sputtered in the velvet dark. The chant of the litany throbbed in the distance, mingling with the slow, steady tolling of the bells.

How many were there crushed together in this

crowd? All Florence, Philip reckoned, as he sat on the chest, waiting for a chance to go through. Then, remembering that Luca's house was in the San Michele quarter, right next to the wall that surrounded the city, he said,

"Mama! Let us go by way of the wall. I am sure that tonight they will let us go that way."

His guess was right. The guard beside the bridge said, "Unless you go that way, you'll never get home. It's all right; the sentries won't bother you."

A flight of steps circled to the platform atop the wall. Lisabetta led the way, holding a small lantern before her.

"Halt! Where are you going?" The sentry was a worried clothmaker, just conscripted into service. He seized the lantern and peered into their faces. Maria, her voice tight with fear, said, "But we were told to come this way. . . ." The sentry relented. "All right. Go ahead. But be careful. There are heaps of cannon balls and canister farther on."

Cautiously they made their way along the rampart. They were exhausted by the time they reached the San Michele quarter. There, the sentry, an old soldier, and therefore calm, helped them down the steep, stone steps.

Lisabetta's lantern picked out an apothecary's sign. Luca's house was flush against the wall.

When Philip knocked at the door, his arm was still shaking from the long strain of carrying the chest. The door opened immediately. Ser Francesco, lantern in hand, rushed out to embrace his wife and children. Maria and the girls cried, then they laughed, and then they cried again. Sometimes one was laughing while the others were still crying. Ser Francesco kept apologizing for not coming after them.

"I could not come for you, for all notaries were conscripted. I wanted to clean up the rooms for you. They are on the top floor—four stories up—three small rooms. But now we are at least inside the walls."

Then Philip's father helped him carry the chest. They stumbled up the narrow, unfamiliar staircase, bumping against the wall and balustrade. At last they reached the tiny apartment. It was a great relief to be rid of the chest. Philip sank wearily onto the floor. Ser Francesco lit four candles and placed them on the table in the center of the big room. Like moths drawn to the light, they all gathered around the table.

Ser Francesco cleared his throat. "Maria, my children . . ." His voice was trembling. "The enemy are but ten leagues distant from Florence. They will attack the city before the week is out." He paused.

"How I racked my brains to decide what was best to do. To stay outside the city means certain capture. To stay inside may mean siege and perhaps starvation. I chose to bring you inside the walls. At least we will all be together. Now let us kneel down in our new home and ask God to help us in the days ahead. Our Father . . ."

When the family prayer was over Philip added one of his own. "Dear God, let no harm come to my father and mother. Protect my sisters. Show me what you want me to do. Mary, my Mother, help me to do it."

At midnight the bells ceased tolling and the street noises melted into the darkness. But it was some time before the Neri family fell into a restless sleep.

The next day Philip was up early. His first thought was to get to confession and prepare himself for Holy Communion. Patriotism demanded that he join in the great public Communion for the safety of the republic. But Philip hardly needed that urging.

At that time many good Catholics went to confession and Communion only once a year. The more pious went once every few months or on great feast days. Only the religious went once a week. Philip himself yearned to receive these sacraments every day, even though he felt he was unworthy of so great a privilege. Hence he felt great joy that he could receive his Lord this extra time.

He went to the Church of San Marco. Fra Benedetto da Foiano was already in his confessional. The friar recognized Philip's voice. Before giving

him absolution he whispered to him, "The time is bad, my son. But God rules all time. Out of evil he can bring good. Love him. Pray to him. Never despair."

Outside the church the heralds were crying the news. "Hear ye! Hear ye! The Grand Council of the People of Florence has decreed that the procession will begin after high Mass at the Cathedral of Our Lady. The fast ends after the procession. Hear ye! Hear ye!"

The heralds' cries rebounded in the still empty streets. Philip decided to go back to Ser Luca's and to attend Mass with his family. He passed by the university. The gates were locked. He wondered whether he would ever be a student there. Next year? Only God knew.

At this moment he did not feel a strong desire to be a university student. True, he loved to read all kinds of books—the poetry of Jacopone da Todi, of his countryman Dante, the joke books of Mainardi. He was a good scholar, or at least Ser Clemente thought he was.

But in his heart of hearts he would rather be like the Blessed John Colombini, the founder of the Gesuati. He was attracted to the life of the hermit—not those who lived on mountain tops, but the poor men who went about in cities, begging for bread, helping the poor, visiting the sick.

The idea of becoming a hermit seemed just to

pop into his head. Up to this time he simply knew what he did not want to be. He did not like business—too much haggling; or law—too much arguing; or his father's profession of notary—too dull. For the religious life—for the priesthood—he had nothing but veneration. But such a life seemed far, far above him, for Philip was as small in his own estimation as he was in size.

Now he was back at the San Michele quarter. In the daylight Ser Luca's house looked as grim as a fortress. Indeed, the thick rectangular walls, the iron-barred embrasures, the battered stone facing—all this told of a time when the house was part of the city's wall of defense. Even now you could not tell where the house ended and the new wall began.

Upstairs his mother and father were waiting for him in the bare center room. "The heralds proclaimed that the procession begins after high Mass", he reminded them. "After that, the fast is over. Shall we go to the cathedral now?"

"We had better if we want to get in", his father said, adjusting his *lucca,* the official robe of the notary. His mother fingered her black lace shawl and straightened the shoulder of her good dress.

"I have put out your doublet and ruff, Philip", she said, pointing to his room. "You, too, must dress for this occasion."

Outside, all Florence seemed to be going to the cathedral. Like the Neris, the people were dressed

in their finest. Guildsmen wore the robes of their trade—scarlet, purple, yellow, and black. The noble families, attended by footmen, were clothed in ermine and many colored velvets. Chains of gold hung from their necks, and they wore rich belts of chased silver studded with gems. Even the servants wore their newest liveries.

Gone was the nervous excitement of the evening before. Now there was a solemn silence in the streets. Perhaps the people were subdued because of the fast. Perhaps they had time to realize the seriousness of the danger that faced them. They knew, too, they were going to the court of the King of Heaven to lay their petitions before him.

The scene at the cathedral added to the air of seriousness, of dignity, of ceremony, of splendor. The archbishop sat on his throne, surrounded by his canons and clergy. Near him sat the members of the Great Council. The high altar gleamed in the soft light of a thousand candles. The choir sang in the purest tones and with a thrilling intensity. Then came the public Communion. As if they were one person, rising by one will, responding to one desire, the people moved forward to the altar to receive the Body and Blood of their Savior.

For hours the Florentines streamed to the altar. When all had received their Lord, the great bronze doors of the cathedral opened and the archbishop led the procession through the streets.

As always in times of peril the people began to

chant the litany of the saints. They called on the Blessed Trinity, on the Virgin Mary, and the saints to free them from sin and deliver them from evil. They recited the Rosary. They sang the *laudi* of Jacopone da Todi. After that, psalms rose on the air like sighs, like sobs, like the eternal lament of all creation. Occasionally there was a pause and someone, a hermit, perhaps, delivered a short fervent sermon.

By one o'clock Philip was exhausted. But, like many others, he was exalted, too. Prayer to God, particularly public prayer, gave him courage. It was not that he believed his prayer forced God to do what he prayed for. Rather he was confident that whatever God willed would be for the best. Still, he did feel that the danger to Florence would pass away.

So, too, did his fellow citizens. After the procession the crowds went home. In a short time fires were lit, the cooking pots began to simmer, and wine began to flow. Cheerful hearts reached for the lute and the guitar. Laughter, gay talk, the high-spirited song so characteristic of Florence floated out over the autumn evening.

On the way up Ser Luca's stairs the Neris met the Bandinis, who occupied the floor beneath. Messer Giorgio Bandini was a goldsmith with a small, fat wife and four roly-poly children. He greeted Ser Francesco with extravagant good humor. "Ser

Luca sent word you were coming. We must have a cup of wine together."

Messer Giorgio would not hear of their refusing either the wine or the supper of roast kid that followed. After supper they sang songs together until the younger children fell asleep in their chairs and Maria, a little shy in a stranger's house, signalled her family that it was time to go upstairs.

That night they all slept soundly. The great public prayer, the proud display of Florence's wealth, power, and unity; the kindness of the Bandinis; the good wine—all these lulled their fears.

Neither they, nor anyone else in Florence, knew that Charles V, king of Spain, king of Italy, emperor of the Holy Roman Empire, the most powerful ruler on earth, was, that very night, dictating a letter to Allesandro de Medici, the deposed tyrant of Florence. The letter concluded:

"I promise you that I shall reduce the rebel Florentines. You shall reign as duke of Florence."

3

SIEGE

THE SPIRIT OF FESTIVITY still clung to the city the next morning, October 13.

Drums and trumpets called up the militia companies. Bravely dressed, armor shining, banners flying, the companies marched in columns of two from their barracks to the ramparts. At the fountains women rested their water jars on their hips and predicted a swift end to the war. One woman, knowing nothing of politics, said that the king of France would come to their aid. "Is he not the enemy of the emperor?"

Another said, "If not the French king, then surely the Genoese will help us."

"We are strong enough to save ourselves", a third woman said, echoing the opinion of her husband who was a lieutenant in the militia.

Small boys with pots for helmets and saucepans for shields played at being soldiers, or helped bring mortar and stone to the masons who were patching cracks in the fortifications. Little girls, pretending they were nurses, bound their little brothers' heads with bandages made from dolls' dresses. No one was really worried.

Philip, too, shared in this general confidence. The council had assigned him to work as a notary's clerk for his father. His job was to keep a careful record of the grain delivered to the public storehouse. A weigher called out the amounts of each load, which Philip listed. Then he gave official receipts to the farmers. To him it seemed there was already enough grain in the bins to feed all Italy. But still it kept pouring in.

Farmers from all the territory around Florence were rushing to the city. By noontime on his first day he had recorded the delivery of 200 bushels of grain. There was no doubt of it: Florence was rich and her people were loyal. Hardly a farmer had failed to make some slurring remark about the enemy, some praise of the city. Philip went home for his dinner with the feeling that the war was practically won.

But, strangely, the mood of optimism disappeared early in the afternoon. One of the farmers dumped a sack of rice on the scales and said, "They're saying that our chief magistrate, the Gonfaloniere Capponi, rode out yesterday with a bodyguard of nobles and sold out to the Medici."

One of the elder notaries came over to Ser Francesco Neri and whispered to him. Philip watched his father's face sadden.

"What is the matter, Father?" he asked.

"Francesco Carducci has been made general", his father said dismally. "It is true the Gonfaloniere Capponi has deserted."

But this was simply the beginning of the evil news. At four o'clock in the afternoon Florentine scouts rode in from the watchtowers outside the city. The imperial army was on the march. There was no time to lose now. Out from the city gates burst messengers to warn the countryside, to deliver urgent messages to Florence's allies, to hurry stragglers lest they fail to reach the city in time. Deputies from the council scurried about the streets summoning the citizens to their duties. All over Florence there was knocking at the door.

"Who knocks?"

"Open in the name of the Great Council."

"What do you want?"

"The council directs you to report immediately to the North Rampart."

"The council directs . . ." These words set the whole city into action. The council directed Philip, since he was too young and too small to bear arms, to remain at the granary during the morning hours. In the afternoons he was to act as a messenger for Captain Hugo D'Onofrio, commanding the Company of the Guild of the Weavers. Philip found Captain D'Onofrio at his station on the west wall. He was a tall, pale man with a long, curving nose. His lower lip hung loosely. It seemed as if his mouth were perpetually opened to give a command. He wore a cuirass of steel, a bronze helmet, and an air of fierce despondency.

The captain looked down at him from his great height.

"So you are Philip Neri, the student, who will run my messages. I have no messages yet, young Philip. Stand close by me and watch that road", he said, pointing ahead of him. "You may see something you never wanted to see."

Philip stared, squinting, into the setting sun. The road appeared white and empty and innocent. After a while Philip heard the faint, dim throbbing of drums.

"It won't be long now", the captain said.

Then, painted against the sun, three horsemen came into view, each clasping a standard in his hand. They sat superb and arrogant, as if they themselves possessed all the power represented by the flags they bore—the imperial standard with its black eagles, the red and gold banner embroidered with the lion and castle of Spain, and the haughty ensign of the Medici.

Behind them came mounted lancers, their spear tips flashing in the sun; after them, four abreast, tall, heavy-set infantrymen with ugly pikes bobbing on their shoulders; and then a regiment of musketeers. The drums beat mercilessly—boom—boom—boom. For a moment Philip felt that the enemy column was a great machine that could march right through thc walls. He cast a fearful glance toward the captain.

"Do not be frightened yet", the captain grimly said. "This is only a parade. They mean to impress us. But the imperial army does not fight like chivalrous knights, all dressed up in tournament clothes. No, when they are ready to fight, you will see scaling ladders, cannon, flaming arrows, ravens. But before you see all that, you will watch their campfires burning many a night. They will wait until we are starving."

When the imperial army came within gunshot of the walls, it broke off into sections, each one taking a position chosen in advance.

"By tomorrow we will be surrounded." The captain spoke as if no one were listening. "It will be a long siege."

Darkness fell. Outside the walls Philip could hear enemy sergeants barking out orders in a strange tongue.

"What language are they speaking?" he asked the captain.

"French. And if you listen closely, you'll hear German, Dutch, Italian, and Spanish, too. They're mercenary troops. They fight for whoever pays them. Two years ago they sacked Rome and put the Pope in peril. They're no different from the Romans who murdered Christ." D'Onofrio's voice was bitter.

The stars came out just as the campfires flamed in the fields beyond the city. Philip was struck by a sudden fancy that the stars were the angels' campfires. Angels surrounded the city as well as the enemy. He was about to tell Captain D'Onofrio about this thought when the soldier suddenly called out to the sergeant.

"Change the guard, Pamfilo", he said. "See to it the men are fed. Philip, get along home. Curfew comes in half an hour."

D'Onofrio rested his hand on Philip's head. "I'm glad you're going to be my messenger. I think we'll get along. Good-night."

"Good-night, captain", Philip said.

Philip soon realized how right was the captain's analysis of the enemy's intentions. Day after day the enemy sat outside the walls, waiting. October faded into November and all the imperial troops did was dig trenches, construct palisades, build wooden towers to observe the city, and make themselves comfortable for the coming winter. From his place by D'Onofrio's side Philip could hear them laughing and talking. It was the same all around the city, as he discovered when he carried the captain's messages to the commanders and magistrates.

At least once a week the enemy made a show of force, discharging cannon burst casually, almost like insolent boys throwing rocks. Frequently heralds came, flying the white flag of truce, and then rumors circled the besieged city that the war was over. But it wasn't over.

Christmas came and there was a week's truce. Both sides laid down their arms and prayed to the Prince of Peace. How strange it was to hear the holy songs rising from the enemy camps—the same songs that the Florentines were singing in their cold, crowded churches. Strangest of all, Alessandro de Medici's captain of horse requested that chaplains be sent from Florence to minister to Italian soldiers! Four Franciscans walked through the wintry sleet to confess the enemies of their city and to sing Mass for them.

For all the fervent patriotism of the Florentines, the remorseless siege began to wear away their spirit of resistance. The great bins of grain were now half-empty. The grain ration dwindled to a measure a day for four people. One by one the horses began to disappear. Wood and charcoal could be used only for cooking. Oil grew scarce.

It was pitiful to watch fat, jolly Messer Bandini shrinking like a lanky wineskin, and his roly-poly children growing as white and skinny as a grandmother's forefinger. Philip's father grew depressed and touchy. Ser Francesco cursed the bitter cold, complained against their damp, drafty quarters. Now he was given to envying the fate of his cousin, Romolo de Neri, who had left Florence the spring before.

"He was wise", Ser Francesco said. "He wanted me to go with him. Romolo is now in San Germano, rich and comfortable, while we starve."

"But Uncle Romolo would help us if he could", Philip said quietly.

Maria, racked with rheumatism, was less complaining. But she could not help worrying about all of them, particularly about the girls. Caterina and Lisabetta were assisting the nuns in the Hospital of San Lorenzo. Twice now they had brought home diseases from nursing the sick—the one a fever, the other a frightening red rash. But mostly Maria prayed all the day through—at Mass in the morning, at home, at vespers. The click of her beads could be heard in the cramped apartment far into the night, and her few precious candles, blessed by the friars, burned one by one before a painted wooden statue of the Virgin.

Philip could not blame people for feeling bitter. Hunger, sickness, anxiety emptied them of all their natural good sense and their festive spirits. But it was horrifying to watch hate take root in their souls. The Florentines now loathed their foes. As February dragged into March they would have gladly died if only the enemy could die with them. Desperate, hotheaded young men demanded that Carducci, the gonfaloniere, plan an attack.

"Better to die fighting than die like rats", they said. But wiser heads restrained them.

"What is the use?" D'Onofrio said to Philip. "Suppose we attack. Perhaps we will break through. But where do we go then? The emperor rules all Italy. No, it is best to sit here and make it so unpleasant for them that they will come to terms. Every day of the siege costs the emperor a thousand florins. When he can no longer pay, the army will melt away."

Spring stole through the siege. The soft breezes, sweet with the scent of forest and meadow, revived the people's faint hopes. At least they would no longer be cold. With the spring came, too, an increasing activity outside the walls. Philip could see the enemy troops dragging cannon to their emplacements. In their rear there was the thud of spades in the sod, the crack of hammer on metal and wood.

One afternoon D'Onofrio suddenly said to Philip, "Now they are *really* serious. You see, they are bringing up their ladders. At the first crack of the cannon you lie flat on the wall. Do not raise your head to see what happens. If I need you I will shout."

A minute later a cannon boomed and Florentine cannon answered. Along the section next to theirs the firing was intense. It kept up all day; the next day it resumed. All through May the enemy smashed relentlessly at the thick walls. Finally came the assault. Protected by their gunfire, a wedge of infantry—some carrying ladders, some pikes—rushed at the wall. The ladders swayed and scraped and hooked into place. Then up sprang the enemy pikemen. Few of them reached the top, for the Florentines, filled with long pent-up fury, hacked at the ladders with axe and halberd and sent the pikemen crashing to the ground. There, stunned and sprawling, the mercenaries were killed by the fire of harquebus and musket. Those who did scale the wall met not one, but several, fatal sword thrusts.

This was but one assault that failed. Others were repulsed to the north and south.

With the beginning of heavy fighting Philip's duties changed. He was no longer needed at the granary, and younger boys were now being used as messengers. But the council needed litter bearers to bring the wounded to the hospitals.

There were wounded every day now, for the attacks continued. The enemy's mines blew up sections of the wall; his cannon tore greater gaps in the rubble. Snipers crept in by night and picked off the unwary.

This new duty as a litter bearer had a strange effect on Philip. After a few days he no longer thought of the siege. Now he was completely absorbed with human beings, with his brothers in Christ. His wounded had become dear to him. He would have given all he had, gladly, to restore their mangled limbs, their broken bodies. He wept with them. He held the hands of dying men. He sang them songs and told them stories. He prayed continuously, not for victory, now, but for the souls of the men who were dying.

Strangely, too, the more deeply Philip became involved with his wounded and the more his heart broke for them, the less anxious he was about himself—or about his future. Man's life in this world was as flimsy as smoke. It vanished in an instant. And then? And then eternity began—either a life of peace with God, or a life of hate and enmity and suffering—a life very much like this bitter war. What mattered, then, was to do God's will here and now. Then even the siege became bearable. The siege too would pass away. The siege too was a wisp of smoke in the light of eternity.

And so the love of God and of man burned ardently in Philip's heart and kept him cheerful, even though he too knew that the city was doomed.

June brought the scent of orange blossoms, but no relief from war. Now even the hardy young men were falling sick from starvation. Yet, whenever the enemy made his assault, the Florentines, with a reckless courage born of desperation, repulsed them with flame, catapults, scalding water, spear showers, stones, and arrows.

Even though the will to resist had been sapped, resistance was now a habit. People thought of dying, but they did not think of surrendering. Even when the heat of July sucked the last feeble springs of strength dry, the city fought on. But there is an end even to the habit of resistance. The time came when weary hands could no longer hold the lance or the sword. On August 12, 1530, Florence fell to the enemy.

When the imperial troops entered the city Philip was with his family in Ser Luca's house. They knelt together before the statue of the Virgin, reciting the Rosary. As they said, "Pray for us sinners now and at the hour of our death", they had reason to believe that this very hour might be the hour of their death. They could hear roaring in the street below. The sack of Florence had begun.

4

FAREWELL TO FLORENCE

IN 1532, TWO YEARS LATER, Philip Neri, now seventeen years old, stood once more in the Dominican Church of San Marco, waiting for Fra Benedetto da Foiano.

How many things had happened during those two years—to Florence, to his family, to himself.

Poor dear Florence—Philip always thought of his city affectionately, as if it were a person. How she had suffered! After the siege, Florence, sacked and bleeding, cowered beneath the boots of the emperor's troops. For two years now, since 1530, Alessandro had been duke of Florence. Florence, the mother of freedom, had become a dukedom—a tyranny!

The Neris had suffered, too, as had a thousand other Florentine families. They had gone hungry. Ser Francesco's profession yielded less and less income. As his father's clerk, Philip knew that well enough. Nevertheless, they had survived, thanks be to God.

Philip, too, in spite of his cheerful disposition, was troubled. He had reached a crossroads in his life and did not know which way to turn. Should he stay in Florence or go away, become a hermit or study at the university? Perhaps Fra Benedetto could help him decide. All Philip's life the Dominican at San Marco had been his support. He had helped prepare him for his first Communion and for confirmation. He was his confessor during the siege, and even after the family had returned to the cottage in San Giorgio.

Philip was so deeply sunk in his own thoughts that he did not notice Fra Benedetto standing beside him.

"Come", the friar said. Philip followed him through a passage to the friary. The friar led him to a small room and motioned him to sit down.

"I received your message", he said to Philip. "You have something to tell me?"

Philip nodded.

The friar was struck by the boy's seriousness.

This was not the gay Pippo he knew so well. Fra Benedetto folded his hands in the sleeves of his habit. Perhaps, he thought, at long last his Pippo had heard God's call to the priesthood. Yet he dared not suggest it. For all Philip's holiness, the boy appeared to love the worldly life. Yet that was not quite the word. Philip was not at all worldly. Far from it. Perhaps it was that he was too innocent to be corrupted by the world; he did not seem to feel thc need of the friary's protecting walls. A shrewd judge of souls, Fra Benedetto rejected this explanation, too. Finally he decided that Philip was so much in love with people that he could not bear to shut himself off from them, from their daily lives, even from their chatter.

"Fra Benedetto . . ." Philip's voice wavered. "My father wants to send me away." He shrugged hopelessly.

"*Ecco!*" the priest exclaimed in surprise. "But why?"

"There is nothing here for me to do, he says. His business affairs are bad. What money he has must go for Lisabetta's dowry. Besides, his cousin—he whom we call Uncle Romolo—has agreed to take me into his business at San Germano. In San Germano there is at least peace. San Germano is under Naples. The Spanish rule there."

"And you do not wish to go?" the friar asked gently.

Philip shook his head.

Fra Benedetto paused. Should he say what was in his mind? He decided he would. "Philip, if you do not want a career in the world, could it be that you are called to another vocation?"

Again Philip shook his head. "I am not sure. I know I love God above everything else. But I do not think I am good enough to be a priest, much less a religious like you, Fra Benedetto."

Suddenly he began to laugh. "Besides, I am so small. I would not reach the top of the pulpit. I should have to preach from a ladder."

"If you are not sure of a religious vocation," Fra Benedetto said, "then you should obey your father. Go to San Germano. Serve your Uncle Romolo as well as you can. San Germano is at the foot of Monte Cassino. Perhaps at the abbey of the Benedictines you will find your true vocation, Pippo. God will reveal it to you if you do as he desires."

"There is nothing to be done then. I shall go. But I shall miss you and San Marco."

"You can write, Pippo. And I shall give you letters to show at our priories in Naples and Rome, should you ever get there."

Philip shook his head. "I don't suppose I ever shall." Then he added, "May I say farewell to San Marco? Will you let me see Fra Angelico's frescoes in the cloister, the chapter room, and the dormitory? Just one last look."

"Of course, Philip."

One last look. Philip devoured the beauty of the frescoes, the peace and quiet of the San Marco friary. On his way out he heard the friars chanting the Office in the choir. At the portal of San Marco, Fra Benedetto said: "Go, my son. Go always with God as he always goes with you."

Tears sprang into Philip's eyes as he knelt for the friar's blessing. "*Addio,* Fra Benedetto. May God reward your kindness to me."

As he walked home Philip felt, if not happier, at least more resigned. Indeed he needed only the assurance that it was God's will for him to obey his father; already his journey seemed less heart-wrenching. He would have liked to make his mark here in Florence if life were not always so turbulent.

These thoughts accompanied him through the city, across the bridge, up the hill of San Giorgio into the pink cottage, a little aged now by wind and rain and sun.

Inside the house his mother called out. "Is that you, Pippo?"

"*Si,* Mama."

She bustled in from the kitchen, eagerly searching his face. "You have talked with Fra Benedetto?"

"Yes."

She gave him a long, questioning look. In her heart she hoped that her Pippo would say yes to the goodness of God and study for the priesthood. She could not bear the thought of his leaving.

"Mama," he said, taking her hands into his own,

whirling her around until she cried out that he would make her dizzy, "Fra Benedetto thinks I should go to Uncle Romolo's."

"Ah, Pippo," she said mournfully, "I will never see you again."

"Who knows, Mama? I may not stay at San Germano. Or I may quickly make my fortune there and return on a great horse."

Even Maria had to laugh at that. It was too ridiculous to imagine Pippo on a great horse. Maria wiped her eyes.

"Well," she said, "if you are going, there is much to be done. I must mend your cloak and bake bread for your knapsack. You must be ready to join the pilgrims setting out for Rome. It is safer to travel in a group; your father said so this morning."

Then Maria began to cry softly—this time because she remembered all the stories she had heard of the hardships of the journey south: of suspicious cities and towns, and the wild robbers who infested the roads, and of the marauding bands of mercenaries.

Ser Francesco nodded briefly when Philip told him of his conversation with Fra Benedetto. "It is best", he said. "There is no hope for you in Florence."

It was not easy to say good-bye to Caterina. She was a full-grown woman now, grave beyond her years.

"I knew it would come at last, little brother. I never believed all this talk about your becoming a notary like Father." Caterina was playing with a small gold ring, her one valuable possession—the gift of her godmother. "I know you have little money, Pippo", she said. "I want you to take this as a remembrance." She held the ring out to him.

Philip's first instinct was to refuse her gift. But, recognizing the loving spirit of her offer, he knew at once that a refusal would rob her of all the satisfaction of her generous impulse. In the years to come it would please her to remember that her kindness had been kindly received. Swiftly he took the ring.

"What a beautiful thought, Caterina. How good of you." He slipped the ring on his small finger. "See, it fits. Or would you rather I wore it as sailors do, in my ear?" Laughing, he kissed her smooth forehead and tugged gently at her lustrous black hair.

Lisabetta seemed to be avoiding a farewell. When he looked at her she would turn her head away quickly. Sometimes she burst into little sobs and ran hastily from the room. Closer to him in age, she felt his coming departure the keenest of all.

The night before he was to leave, Philip tried to cheer Lisabetta by playing the merry tune of the Roman travellers on the guitar. Soon her full rich voice picked up the song. When the song had rinsed her sadness away, Philip jumped up and said quickly, "Won't you climb San Giorgio hill with me? I would love to see the city from the top of the hill—one last time."

"Of course, Pippo." Lisabetta picked up a shawl.

Together, humming songs, they clambered up the hill. When they reached the top Lisabetta said, "Ah, Pippo, you knew I wanted to be alone with you a moment before you left, didn't you? There is so much I want to say that I don't know how to say it all."

"And I wished for this moment too, Lisabetta", Philip said. "Who knows when I may return? It is in God's hands. I would like to have stayed to see you married. Who will it be?" Lisabetta blushed. The wind stirred her hair. "Messer Cini, I think."

"You love him best?" She nodded.

"I'll pray that your wish is God's wish and that he grants it. Promise me, Lisabetta, that you will look after our parents." She nodded again. Somehow, he knew, Lisabetta was the right manager for the family, even though she was the youngest.

"Lisabetta," he said playfully, "what is your dearest wish in all the world? Look, look down on Florence. Suppose you could claim anything the city possessed. What would you want?"

Lisabetta frowned slightly and pursed her lips. Then she said, "A dress of gold cloth. And you, Philip?"

"I would want the sky of Florence. See how lovely it is—clear and soft, hanging like a light veil over the Duomo, the Campanile, the Badia, the towers of the Bargello and of the Signoria." Philip pointed to the Siena gate. "Look over there. It is there I shall meet the pilgrims tomorrow after Mass."

Tomorrow he would be gone. A dim presentiment that he would never see Florence again made him shiver.

"*Addio,* my Florence", he whispered, "fairest city in the world. May the guardians of your gates, the Madonna, Saint Leonard, and Saint George, restore your liberty and peace."

Philip slept little that night. Towards dawn he decided to dress. The house was full of quiet sounds. The others were up too.

Together, in silence, the family went to Mass at San Giorgio's. In silence they returned to the house, hugging their sorrow to their hearts. There were a few choked words during breakfast. When they had finished eating, Maria stuffed Philip's knapsack with a large loaf of bread, some dried figs, a smoked rind of pork, a lump of rock salt, a yellow cheese as round and hard as a cannon ball, a string of white onions, and a flask of wine.

Philip strapped the bag on his shoulders. Now he was ready to go. He embraced his sisters and his mother. Maria, her task finished, suddenly was unstrung. Her shoulders sagged; the blood drained from her face. Silently she wept.

Ser Francesco was talking loudly to comfort them all. "You will be better off with Uncle Romolo", he said encouragingly. "You will restore the family fortune." He gave Philip his blessing and embraced him.

Philip turned to the door, his heart pounding furiously. He, too, felt like weeping. "God help me", he thought. "May I be half again as worthy as they think I am." But he did manage to muster a smile.

Outside he took one last look at his family and his home. "Thank you, thank you all." He kissed his hand to them. Then he turned swiftly and ran down the hill. Once he was out of their sight he let the tears pour down his face.

At the Siena Gate six pilgrims waited for him. The leader of the band, an old man with a scraggly beard and deeply sunken cheeks, welcomed him. He looked approvingly at Philip's threadbare pilgrim's cloak and his slender knapsack. Good, the lad was aware that their journey was to be one of penance.

"We shall be begging our way before long. Come, let us start. You have many leagues to go, little brother."

The old man leaned on his staff and knelt on the stones. Philip and the others joined him.

"*Jesu cum Maria sit nobis in via*—May Jesus and

Mary be with us on the way." They crossed themselves and rose.

Silently, two by two, the pilgrim party passed through the arched gate out onto the road to Siena. Philip would be with them for more than a month as they walked from Florence to Siena, to Assisi, to Montepulciano, and thence to Orvieto, Viterbo, and Tivoli where he would part company with them. They would go to Rome, he to Subiaco and thence to San Germano.

"God wills it", Philip said to himself. He felt less sad now that he was on his way. But he did not trust himself to look back over his shoulder at Florence.

5

PHILIP TRIES TO BE A MERCHANT

PHILIP SAT DOWN under a eucalyptus tree that grew beside the road and watched his pilgrim companions go off on their way to Rome. What good companions they had been! Had it not been for them would he now know so many tales of the noble saints of Tuscany and Umbria? True, they had suffered together, too. Once Philip had eaten no more than an onion in three days.

But the keenest of all his memories were those of the evenings under the stars. Often, on frosty nights, he lay huddled in his cloak, gazing at the heavens. The million stars, all bright as angels, made him feel very lonely and insignificant. They reminded him that man was a pilgrim whose life was brief and whose true home was heaven. Yet he was grateful for his loneliness, for it gave him more time to listen to God's voice speaking to him through his own prayers. Often he heard a voice within him say:

"Do you love me, Philip?"

"Yes, Lord."

"Do you trust me?"

"With all my heart."

"Will you accept whatever I desire you to do?"

"Yes, Lord. Let me know your will and I will do it. Am I not now doing what you want me to do?"

Philip waited and listened. But he heard only the sighing of the wind through the poplars and the muted noises of the night. He had the feeling that God was leading him on his journey as a father leads a small son.

"You will see, you will see what I want you to do. But first I must take you away from your home—the people and places and things you have learned to love. You must learn to give up what you love for my sake. You must learn to love them in a new way."

How quickly one learned that lesson under the stars. Philip wondered whether he had not been too attached to Florentine ways. The stars and the angels were not Florentines. They belonged to all

Italy—not only to Italy, but to Europe; not only to Europe, but to the whole world.

He was becoming aware of how much more intensely he could love God. In the quiet nights he began to realize that, while he had always hated sin, he had not yet—not by many leagues—arrived at the state he so often begged to achieve, that state in which "My God and my all" would be a fact, rather than an aspiration.

"When, O Lord, shall I love you as I ought?"

"In due time, my son."

"As you wish, Lord. But may it come soon." Soon, Philip felt, God would let him know just what he should do.

He picked up his almost empty knapsack, rose to his feet, patted the trunk of the friendly eucalyptus tree, and, with a firm stride, set out for San Germano. He sang aloud to keep his spirits up.

By good fortune he overtook an empty farm cart drawn by two oxen. The driver, a peasant, was sleepily prodding his great beasts.

"Hello", Philip called out. "Are you by chance going to San Germano?"

The driver nodded.

"May I ride with you awhile?" he asked.

"Get on", the driver said. "The oxen won't feel the difference." The man laughed boisterously. "I'd guess you don't weigh as much as your shadow. Ha, ha!"

The driver himself was small and fat, and his

face shone as though good olive oil and wine were seeping through his pores.

Philip leaped on the wagon. "It's good to be small and skinny", he said. "It takes less to fill your stomach or cover your bones. It's more economical."

The driver slapped his round, firm belly. "Say what you will, my little sparrow, I'd rather be fat than lean as you are. You can't travel on an empty stomach. To whose house do you go in San Germano, foreigner?"

"To my uncle's, Romolo de Neri's. I come from Florence", Philip said.

The driver turned to stare at him, a cautious, appraising look in his eyes. "Your uncle is a rich man", he said admiringly. "He will feed you well. The Florentines are all rich."

"Not all Florentines", Philip said lightly. "I myself have but three *giulios* left."

"If you are not rich now, you will become rich", the driver said firmly. "All Florentines grow rich. The Pope is a Florentine. The Florentines are richer than the lord abbot of Monte Cassino whom I serve."

The driver prodded the oxen with his goad. "Go Cosmas, go Damian. We shall never get home."

That night Philip slept by fits and starts in the wagon alongside the fat little driver. Tomorrow he would be at Uncle Romolo's. Tomorrow a new life would begin. Would it be tomorrow that God would reveal his new manner of life, too? He shivered, partly from cold, partly from excitement.

The day broke at last. Philip was so eager to be on his way that he did not even want to spare the time for breakfast—two dried figs, a bite of smoked pork, and a mouthful of water. But the driver—Carlo his name was—wouldn't think of moving until he had eaten well from his basket and fed the oxen their bundles of hay.

"Ecco," said Carlo, belching, "do you want to run up and down mountains instead of riding comfortably? Be patient, Messer Shadow," he said. "Here, eat some of this." Carlo offered Philip a wedge of his loaf.

"Thank you, Carlo. Thank you", Philip said. He took one bite and slipped the rest into his sack.

Eventually they did start. The wagon rumbled and creaked on its great wooden wheels. Cosmas and Damian lurched forward in short, convulsive heaves. At what a slow pace the miles were eaten up! When they climbed the shoulder of a great mountain Carlo pointed to a valley huddled below.

"San Germano", he said.

Philip felt he had never seen so fair a sight. Below him the red tiled roofs had just picked up the sun. To his left, crowning a high ridge, sat the enormous monastery of Monte Cassino. Here, more than 1,000 years before, Saint Benedict of Nursia had come with his companions to found an order that preserved Christian learning during centuries of war, pestilence, and decay.

Monte Cassino! How often Philip had heard this melodious name chime like sweet bells from the pulpit of Santa Croce. Now the holy mountain, crowned by its stern, fortresslike monastery, seemed to Philip a middle heaven. He had the feeling that hosts and hosts of angels were mounted on this high fortress of God, ready to swoop at the bidding of God's will to the help of souls struggling in the valley below.

As the wagon made its slow descent Philip kept his eyes on Monte Cassino. Maybe this was his destination. Perhaps he would become a monk. Then he recalled his old wish to become a hermit. He was so preoccupied that he scarcely noticed they were already near the town.

On closer view the town of San Germano itself looked cramped and small. It was crowded, too, with loaded wagons, and burdened donkeys, and men babbling prices.

"It is the day the merchants from Gaeta display their wares", Carlo explained. "It is a day your uncle will be very busy."

Philip found his Uncle Romolo at the fountain in the center of the town. He had bade Carlo good-bye, thanked him, and pressed one of his last three *giulios* upon him, which Carlo pocketed without a word. A little dazed by the hubbub, jostled by the busy crowd, Philip hugged the walls of the narrow street and made his way to the open space around the fountain.

Uncle Romolo looked no different than he had during his last visit to Florence. He was talking in sharp, barking Neapolitan to a dark-skinned man with a long, curving nose.

Philip waited until the haggling was over and the two men had touched hands in a sign of agreement. Then he said, "Uncle Romolo."

Romolo de Neri spun around. "Pippo! Bless my soul. Have you just arrived? Are you well?" There was a touch of anxiety in his voice.

"Very well, thanks be to God", Philip began. "I rode in a wagon almost all the way from Tivoli."

"Ah, Pippo, it is good you are here. But now you must be tired. Why don't you get along home? It is on the Via Reale. You can rest there. I shall come as soon as I can."

Philip found the Casa Neri without trouble, for the gates were adorned with the Neri coat of arms—an azure shield marked by three gold stars. His aunt came to meet him, stretching out her fat, graceless arms in welcome.

"Pippo, Pippo. We have been expecting you for weeks. Let your Aunt Giovanna give you a kiss. Come into the house. Oh, we are glad to see you."

Inside, his room was ready. New clothes—a little

too large for him—were taken from closets and chests. A manservant brought hot water for his bath. And all the time Aunt Giovanna's conversation rambled! Yet there was a single sentiment that bound up all her scattered remarks on the weather, the government at Naples, her husband's many occupations as a trader, a banker, a renter of farms, a local magistrate, an agent for the lord abbot of Monte Cassino. She kept referring to the sad fact that Romolo had no son to carry on his name or to take over his enterprises.

"Ah, Pippo, we will treat you like a son. Here at Casa Neri you will want for nothing. Messer Romolo will not even compel you to work. Do not think of it. Read, study, write poems. We will make you good and fat. All we will ask is that you learn how to use the inheritance that will be yours when we are gone."

Her dark, beady eyes darted all around him. He could not move without her jumping up to anticipate his wish. "A sweet? A cup of chocolate? You wish to rest?"

Quickly she rose and almost ran out of his room, calling out loudly to the servants, "Do not disturb Messer Filippo. He is resting."

Then she was back in a second with cushions for his bed. Her maternal affection cascaded upon him. "Is there anything more I can do for you?"

Inwardly Philip groaned. If she does any more

for me I am surely done for, he thought. "Nothing, Signora. I am overwhelmed by your kindness." That was the right expression, he could tell, for she smiled happily at him.

"Tonight a feast in your honor. Pheasant and rice, hares, and a joint of veal. I must go now to help in the kitchen."

Uncle Romolo came home late in the afternoon. He greeted his wife and then came immediately to Philip's room.

"Have you rested?" he asked heartily. "It will take a week or two of long sleeping to take the ache out of your bones. The last time I came home from Florence I slept for a month. But you'll be feeling fit soon. Green bones don't ache like old ones."

His uncle and aunt forced him to eat. Philip, now used to nibbles of the simplest foods and the merest trickle of wine, tried hard to do justice to the delicacies they placed before him.

"Have more pasta, Filippo", Aunt Giovanna urged.

"Try this sweet", Uncle Romolo said. "There are none like it in Florence."

Uncle Romolo kept talking as his nephew tried to eat. He told Philip of his long friendship with his father, of his early days as a merchant, of his recent successes in business.

Philip's head drooped. His eyes grew heavy. He

had to call on his reserves of strength to keep awake and to answer Uncle Romolo's questions about Florence. He felt that he was trapped.

Why should he feel trapped? He asked himself that question a dozen times in the next few weeks. Why should all this affection, all this generosity, oppress him and make him long to run away? Surely he was not ungrateful. He did not dislike Uncle Romolo or Aunt Giovanna. He could not complain of the "work", which consisted of accompanying Uncle Romolo on his daily rounds, of copying accounts, and of writing some letters in a fair hand.

Moreover, eager as they were to have him near them, his uncle and his aunt were not prying. They not only allowed him to take long walks and to make new friends; they encouraged him to do so.

"You must go to see Dom Anselmo", Uncle Romolo would say. "He is the choirmaster at the abbey. You will enjoy talking to him about music."

"You must make the acquaintance of the Cavalier Sebastiano, the royal podesta", his aunt would say.

Smiling, they would wish him a happy visit and beg him to enjoy himself.

He found relief from their attentions only in the hours of prayer in his room, in the moments during Mass. "Dear God," he said, "if you will that I stay at San Germano, help me to bear it."

6

A PILGRIMAGE TO GAETA

After he had been at San Germano a few weeks Philip, still uneasy, made up his mind to reveal his discontent to Dom Anselmo. He had grown to know the monk well and trusted his judgment. When he had explained his problem the Benedictine shook his head knowingly.

"Dear son," he said, "you may be discontented because you are homesick. Absence from home makes one unhappy because, like heaven, home is a place where we can rest in the possession of all that we love. Once I was sent to Rome to prepare the choir at St. John's to sing the Easter Mass.

Yet in Rome, of all places, I wept—for Monte Cassino. I dreamed of my cell here, which seemed sweeter than the Garden of Eden. Even Roman food had a sour taste. I was sick for home."

Philip shook his head. "I do not think I am homesick for Florence", he said.

Dom Anselmo looked at him thoughtfully. "You are not ill?"

"No—not at all. I am too well."

"Then perhaps your angel disturbs your soul because you are not doing what God desires." The monk paused for a moment and then continued. "Have you heard of the holy grotto at Gaeta? It is high on a cliff. You will find the shrine of the Trinity between the sides of a rock which is said to have split apart the day our Lord died on Calvary. Many of our fathers and brothers have gone there to meditate and pray. They come back refreshed in soul. Go there, my son. If you do not then find peace, come to me again. But go there first."

That night Philip told his uncle and aunt of Dom Anselmo's advice.

Uncle Romolo pulled at his beard and looked at his wife. Giovanna shrugged her shoulders.

"It is a day's journey", Uncle Romolo said. "The Grotto of the Santa Trinita is outside Gaeta. It is hard to reach."

"But I have walked all the way from Florence", Philip said. "It will take no more than one day to reach Gaeta—even less if you will lend me a mule or a donkey. Please, uncle."

Philip's face, indeed his whole slender body, was quivering with eagerness.

"It is near Christmas. Why not wait until after Christmas? It is not the best time of year to travel", Aunt Giovanna said.

"No, no", Philip said ardently. "It is a very good time, Aunt Giovanna. Besides," he added, "I will pray for you at Santa Trinita."

Uncle Romolo remained silent. How delightful, yet how strange his nephew was. Ever since Philip had lived in his house life had taken on a new zest. Even now he felt his heart swelling with pride at the thought that Philip would become his son and heir. Indeed, he had hinted as much in the marketplace, and he was flattered by the response his hints had brought forth.

"Such a kind young man, so courteous", people said.

Philip attracted people. Friends who had been stand-offish now made a point of stopping by to visit. Why, only last night his house had been filled with music, as gay as a prince's palace. Philip had played the guitar and had sung one song after another—gay Florentine songs that his neighbors in San Germano had never heard before.

Hence he was reluctant to let Philip go, even for so worthy a reason as a visit to Santa Trinita.

For a second he thought of accompanying him on his pilgrimage. But then, remembering how inaccessible the grotto was, he put the idea aside.

"Very well, Philip, you may go", he said finally.

"Tomorrow, tomorrow", Philip shouted enthusiastically.

"And you shall have a mule, too", Romolo said.

"Thank you, uncle."

Later, in the privacy of their own chamber, Giovanna said to her husband, "Do you think Philip is truly happy with us?"

"Giovanna! How can you doubt it?" Romolo was shocked. "Has he not been extremely amiable?"

Giovanna sighed. "Most amiable", she said. Again she sighed.

"What troubles you, my wife?" Romolo was accustomed to Giovanna's sudden anxieties.

"Philip is not meant for San Germano", she said sorrowfully. "He is like a small, lost bird. He is happy, but he longs for his own garden. Soon he will fly away."

"Nonsense", Romolo growled. "Where would he go?"

"I do not know", Giovanna said. "But he will go."

"Woman's talk."

Romolo pretended he did not believe her. Yet he, too, was deeply concerned. He already knew that Philip did not relish the life of a merchant. Irritably he said, "I wish you would not mention his leaving, Giovanna."

Giovanna did not answer until she had finished her Rosary. "You will soon see if I am right", she said.

The next morning Philip set out for Gaeta. It was a cold, bleak day, but his heart sang. He prodded the mule's flanks with his heels and pulled at one of its long, floppy ears.

"The sooner you get there the sooner you'll get back, Messer Mule."

Within the hour the rain came, cold and cutting, but such was the ardor in Philip's heart that he hardly felt it at all. At the fifth milestone he paused to rest his mule. Then he plunged on. At the tenth milestone he stopped again and ate the lunch Aunt Giovanna had prepared for him.

It was late in the afternoon when he came near to Gaeta. He felt that he would recognize the holy mountain from Dom Anselmo's description, but, to be safe, he asked a herdsman for directions.

The man peered up at him, unwilling to open the hood of his woolen cloak more than a crack.

"What! The Holy Rock! Are you crazy, sir, in this weather? Bear to your left at the next crossroads. God keep you."

Philip thanked him and rode away. He followed the path to the base of the mountain. Then he tethered the mule and gave the beast a bag of oats.

He raced up the footpath. In a few minutes, however, he had to slacken his pace, for the climb was steep, and the path, although well marked by the monks, was slippery in the rain. He wondered how many others had climbed this hill to find peace.

Near the summit the path ended abruptly against a massive wall of rock. He looked above him. Yes, there it was—an iron ladder leading up to a great crack in the rock. Unhesitatingly Philip began to scale the steep cliff. Grasping the upper rungs with his hands, he heaved himself up, step by step, for he was tired now and he felt a little giddy after his rapid ascent.

Finally, panting for breath, he reached a table of rocks that covered a split in the mountain. Directly before him was a circular chapel that seemed to grow out of the rock floor.

When he had caught his breath Philip entered the chapel. It was so dark he could barely see the crucifix on the altar. When his eyes grew used to the darkness, he saw the crude furnishings—two candles, almost burned out, a censer, a missal wrapped in waxed cloth, a lectern, and a pair of dusty cruets.

For all its solitude the chapel did not seem empty. On the contrary, it was overwhelmingly filled with the presence of God. Even if he had not known of the tradition that the rock had split during the earthquake at our Lord's death, Philip felt he would have recognized the sanctity of the place.

He fell to his knees. "Lord, here I am", he said. In the silence of his soul he heard a voice say, "I have been waiting for thee, Philip."

Now began for Philip an indescribable moment—yet moment was not the word for it because time ceased and an enormous quietness possessed him. He felt his heart swell with love as he kept saying silently, "Yes, Lord" to the whispering in his soul.

In a flash he recalled the gospel story of the rich young man who had asked our Lord what he should do to be saved, and our Lord's answer, "Keep the commandments." And then he heard the young man say that he had kept the commandments all his life, and our Lord then said, "Sell thy goods, give to the poor and follow me."

At first he did not realize that the gospel story was pointed at himself. He was not rich. He had no money. Ah, but he *was* rich—if not in actual goods, then in the possibility of owning them. And was he not even now, despite his profession to love God above all his creatures, actually preparing to spend his life in pursuit of earthly things?

Philip began to weep. As the tears came he sobbed aloud, "Oh, Lord, I have been a wretch. All my life long you have been calling me to come to you and follow you. And I have never had the courage to do so. You wanted me, and I hung back. I have wanted you and you alone, but I never took the steps to reach you. All you ask is the gift of myself. I give you everything—all the love I have for my parents, my studies, my city of Florence, myself. I desire you alone. To desire anything but you is madness. Oh, why have I waited so long to say this?" Bewailing his indecision, his yielding to circumstances, he fell on the ground.

"Dear Lord Jesus," he prayed, "you have given me all that I am. More, you have given me yourself. I am nothing but what you have given me. I am empty. Give me yourself. Make me yours."

For a long time the tears came. In his present state all his years seemed a great waste. False piety, a pretense of loving God without completely abandoning himself to God's will—that's what he had practiced. But from now on things would be different.

"I promise, Lord, I give you my word. I vow it. If you will accept the vow, I will do what you demand of me. Do but show me what you wish me to do."

He waited in the great silence of the chapel. Outside the wind died down. He felt his heart smash against his ribs as though it were a soul eager to fly to heaven. An indescribably sweet strength poured through his veins, buoyed up his body.

Prostrate on the floor, he nevertheless seemed to float on air. Or rather, held in strong arms, he was being rushed at incredible speed through oceans of light.

Was he asleep? His senses seemed sealed. He neither felt, nor heard, nor saw, nor tasted, nor smelled. He was not even thinking. Yet he was intensely alive. Never had he been more alive in his life. Indeed, compared to this moment all his past life was gray, dull, and lifeless. Philip was at rest in the heart of God.

Gradually, like a man coming out of a deep sleep, Philip was born to himself again. He felt his heart throb. The rough cold stone of the floor chafed his forehead. His bones ached from the cold. He smelt the musty damp of the chapel. Outside a bird's note hovered on the soft wind.

Rising to his feet, Philip rubbed his eyes and yawned. A streak of light pierced the darkness of the chapel, striking a spark from a vein of quartz in the altar stone. Startled, Philip looked out. Yes, it *was* the dawn, faint yet clear, in the eastern sky, a small red stain spreading slowly over the ocean of air. He knelt, said a short prayer, and scrambled down the iron ladder.

"Oh, my poor mule", he thought. "May the angel of this place protect him. What will Uncle Romolo say if he is lost?" But the mule was exactly where he had tethered him. The lonesome beast greeted him with a queasy bray and stamped his hoof in his eagerness to be gone.

Philip struck out into the rising sun. As he rode home, the way of his life stretched out before him as clear and straight as the road the Romans had laid out hundreds of years before.

"I shall go to Rome", Philip heard himself saying. "I shall go to the heart of the Church, to the city of Peter. I shall go as a hermit. I shall work and pray and do what the Lord shows me I should do."

All the way back to San Germano birds sang as if it were spring.

When he arrived at the Casa Neri Philip told his uncle and aunt of his decision.

"I shall be leaving for Rome", he said. "I am sure that is what God wants."

Somehow Philip felt that they, too, had shared his experience at Santa Trinita. But they hadn't. They were astounded and sad. Uncle Romolo's face twisted with grief. Aunt Giovanna rolled her eyes and fussed with her neck cloth.

"But surely, Philip, this decision is too important to be rushed. . . . Your father must be consulted. If you wish to do good, stay here and earn your fortune. You will have more to give to the poor. . . . Have you spoken about this to Dom Anselmo?"

"I am your guardian, Philip. I cannot permit it."

Thus the good people argued, far into the night, certain that Philip was leaving only because, in some way they could not understand, they had offended him and driven him away.

To all their arguments and entreaties, even to their tears, Philip replied that it was God's will. Finally he did convince them that he loved them dearly.

"I owe my conversion to you", he said. "Truly. If I had not come to San Germano, I would never have met Dom Anselmo. I would never have reached the Santa Trinita. It is your goodness that brought me here and that now sends me to Rome."

"Ah," said Romolo, "you do not know Rome. You will be disappointed. Rome is not what you imagine it to be."

"Nevertheless, uncle, I go to Rome."

Philip kissed his relatives tenderly and slipped away to his room. On his way out he heard Aunt Giovanna say, "You see, Romolo, I told you he would not stay . . ."

7

PHILIP GOES TO ROME

IT WAS THE DAY before Christmas, 1533, that Philip first saw Rome. He was walking as fast as he could along the Latin Way, fearful that he would not reach the Eternal City in time for the midnight Mass at St. Peter's. Rome was drawing him like a magnet. Never before had he felt so eager to be at a certain place, nor so sure that he was going to discover there his destiny, his goal, his place in God's mysterious plan.

Suddenly he looked up and there was Rome—the center of the world. Directly ahead of him was the ancient *Porta Latina,* the Latin Gate. Beyond the gate the Palatine Hill, cluttered with rubble, looked down on the ruins of the Colosseum, the temple of Claudius, the remains of the Forum. To the right, looming over the walls, was the immense Basilica of St. John Lateran. Slightly to his left were three hills, the Aventine, the Gianiculo, and, in the distance, the Vaticano.

It was just as Uncle Romolo had said. If he stayed on the Latin Way, he would go right past the tomb of the Scipio, the baths of Caracalla; thence through the Circo Massimo to the Temple of Vesta. Then he would cross the Tiber by way of the Palatine Bridge and follow the river bank until he reached the Castle of San Angelo. From that point he could see St. Peter's.

His heart quickened again at the thought that soon he would be at the tomb of Saint Peter. Redoubling his steps hc bent forward against the keen winter wind. Soon hc was within the city. He looked about him curiously, expecting to be struck by the grandeur of the ancient capital as he had pictured it. But the streets were deserted. Great heaps of stones littered the Latin Way. Burned out buildings stared vacantly at prowling dogs, grunting swine, and a few shivering wayfarers.

Never mind, he told himself. It will be better in the center of the city. It was a little better. Some of the great palaces had a lived-in look. The people were better dressed and a few lords and ladies were carried in luxurious sedan chairs by porters. But Rome seemed no longer an imperial capital. It was a patched-up ruin. Like Florence, Rome, too, was paralyzed by war and its aftermath—the sack, pestilence, and poverty.

As he passed the Arch of Constantine, Philip saw a small, bearded man kneeling before a makeshift wooden cross. Dressed in a coarse brown woolen robe, a crucifix dangling from his neck, the man was praying aloud. When Philip approached him the man cried out, "Ye who enter Rome beware of sin. See what sin has done to the imperial city. The houses are empty, the churches are fallen down, the poor are not fed. Repent! Give alms!"

Philip stared at this strange figure. Could this man be a hermit? He had heard that many of the hermits of Rome wore monastic robes and preached in the streets.

"Are you a hermit?" Philip asked.

"I am Bernardino, the hermit", the man replied. "And you? Are you a pilgrim?"

"I have come to Rome to be a hermit myself", Philip said. "I have no place to live, nor any money. My first wish is to hear the midnight Mass at St. Peter's."

Bernardino sprang from his knees and embraced Philip. "Come with me", he said.

As they approached the Church of San Girolamo

the hermit explained, "Here is a place where hermits are welcome. There is a guest house where we can rest and wash, for San Girolamo is the headquarters of the Confraternity of Charity."

Philip was happy to find out that Rome, too, had confraternities—those societies of laymen and priests who took care of pilgrims and travelers, of the sick and the poor. The very name—Confraternity of Charity—excited him. Perhaps he could join this confraternity.

San Girolamo was exactly the kind of church Philip loved. It was small, with a walled cloister next to it, just like the little Franciscan chapels with their attached convents that dotted the hills in his native Tuscany. He was not at all surprised when Bernardino told him that San Girolamo had once belonged to the Franciscans but was now staffed by chaplains of the confraternity.

In the vestibule of the church he saw a painting of Saint Francis of Assisi in ecstasy. Inside, a knot of men were keeping the vigil of Christmas by making the Stations of the Cross. Philip's heart leaped. Here was the Rome he dreamed of, the Rome that was Christ's second home. They fell on their knees before the Blessed Sacrament. Philip thanked God for inspiring him to speak to the hermit and for bringing him to San Girolamo.

Bernardino touched Philip's shoulder and motioned him to follow. He led Philip to a side door that opened on the cloister. Again Philip's heart leaped, for here, too, was a place that was strangely familiar—as if he had once been here, or had dreamed of being here. There was a tiny garden with a fountain in the center, an orange tree in one corner, and, against the wall facing the street, a rock garden that waited only for the kiss of spring to wake up and dance with color.

The old monastery itself faced two sides of the garden. The walls of the upper story were dotted with small, square, cell-like windows, while those of the lower story were broken by low, open arches. The whole enclosure made him feel that prayer had breathed a spirit of joy and peace into the stones, the fountain, and the garden.

They crossed the garden and entered the guest house, the old chapter room of the friars. Inside the door Philip saw a few old men stretched out on beds of straw. An oil lamp flickered beneath a picture of Saint Paula. Above the picture Philip read, "On this site once stood the house of the noble Roman lady, Saint Paula, mother of the poor. Here, too, the illustrious Doctor of the Church, Saint Jerome, visited and preached to the early Christians." No wonder, he thought, there is an air of holiness about San Girolamo.

He had finished washing and was resting on the fresh straw when Bernardino said, "Brother pilgrim, I will leave you now. On my way out I will tell Persiano Rosa that you are here. Messer Persiano is a layman, a member of the confraternity, who has charge of the guest house."

In a few minutes a short, stocky man, his face brimming with tranquil joy, burst into the room. He grasped Philip's hands and pressed them heartily.

"You are welcome to San Girolamo", he said. "Have you eaten? Where are you from? What is your name? Do you plan to stay? Have you any way of supporting yourself in Rome?"

When Philip answered these and a dozen other questions Persiano's face grew troubled.

"I wish I could say that you could stay here. But the confraternity receives only travellers and pilgrims. Much as I regret it, you can remain here only a week. However," he added cheerfully, "something will turn up. There are as many Florentines in Rome as ants in a bowl of sugar. The Florentines help each other. And, if your mind is set on being a hermit, there's precious little money they'll need to give you. Welcome again, Philip Neri. I shall see you tomorrow." With a cheerful smile and a wave of his hand Persiano Rosa disappeared.

All the way to St. Peter's Philip kept thinking of his remarkably good fortune. He had reached Rome in time for Christmas. The hermit had brought him to the one place of shelter in the city. Gratitude filled Philip's heart as he entered the Cathedral of St. Peter well before midnight. He knelt for a while before the tomb of Saint Peter, made his confession to one of the canons in a side chapel, and then found a place alongside a pillar.

Now the church was beginning to fill up. The soft candlelight shone on the richly veined marble and the gold and silver ornaments of the high altar. The sacred music began. A thousand voices, it seemed, heralded the Savior's birth. People began to murmur, "They are coming. The procession is coming."

First acolytes and priests in cassocks and surplices, then bishops and cardinals in purple and scarlet emerged from the shadows. Finally, preceded by his noble guards, the Holy Father himself, wearing white and gold vestments and the triple crown upon his head, moved solemnly up the aisle.

During the solemn Pontifical Mass Philip thought of Bethlehem. He was in the cave, kneeling before the infant Savior. He whispered, "Oh, my Jesus, all-powerful God who became a child for our sakes, help me to be your child. I have come to Rome to do your will. What do you wish me to do? I give you my heart. Do with it as you will. Do you want me simply to pray? To beg? To preach to the poor? Anything you ask, Lord, anything."

When he received Communion that night Philip

felt a surge of great trust in God. He believed that God had answered his prayer and that he had granted all the graces Philip needed to become a hermit in Rome. His heart heard a voice inside him say, "Trust me, Philip, and follow me in all things. I will lead you to heaven. Only trust me, Philip."

Philip slept that night on a straw mattress at the guest house of San Girolamo. He woke up early the next morning, Christmas Day, and, after sponging the sleep from his eyes, he crossed the garden and entered the church by way of the cloister door. Morning Mass was about to begin. Philip resolved to offer this Mass as a thanksgiving for the graces he had received the night before. He bowed his head in prayer.

When he looked up he saw Persiano Rosa, the guest master, kneeling beside him. When Mass was finished his new friend tapped him on the shoulder and whispered, "Come with me."

Outside, Persiano Rosa said, a smile wreathing his open face, "Do you believe in miracles?"

"Of course", Philip said, smiling in return.

"Well, here is another one you can thank God for. Last night, when I left you, I went to the house of Galeotto del Caccia, the director of Customs, to collect clothes for the Confraternity of

Charity. As we talked, I mentioned that a fellow Florentine named Philip Neri had arrived at the guest house and that he wanted to be a hermit. Messer Galeotto is a great man, a rich man, and a generous one. Without blinking an eye he said, 'Send him to me.' "

Persiano laughed out loud at Philip's look of amazement. "So, young Philip Neri, get you around to Ser Galeotto's house on the Plaza Sant' Eustachio, a stone's throw in that direction"—he pointed—"and I have no doubt you will have a bed and crust of bread in exchange for some small service or other."

"God bless you, Messer Rosa", Philip said fervently. He was a little stunned at the sudden answer to his prayers. He went back to the guest house for the shoulder bag that contained his books and linen and then set out for Ser Galeotto's house.

He found it too quickly, he thought, for the shutters were still closed and there was no sign of life in the tall building. Philip decided to wait outside until someone opened the bronze doors, for he did not want to disturb the household at so early an hour. He went to the fountain in the middle of the square and sat beside it.

The wintry sun suddenly burst through the gray sky, turning the jets of water from silver into gold. He scooped up a handful of the sun-flecked water.

It tasted cold and sweet. Beside him two turquoise-streaked pigeons pecked at the water, clucking to each other. He heard, too, the chirp of a covey of sparrows and, then, less distinctly, a faint, desolate mew. That was no bird. It was like the cry of a tiny lost sheep.

He looked about him and saw nothing. But when he bent down he found, huddled at his feet, a quivering orange and white kitten. Philip picked it up, and felt the kitten's nerves coil and uncoil and heard a faint humming purr. The kitten's tiny claws clung to the rough cloth of his cloak. He was so absorbed in its antics that he did not notice the doors of Galeotto del Caccia's house open. Two boys, one about eight and the other eleven, spied him and padded to his side.

"My, you're a pretty one", Philip was saying to the kitten. "What innocent gray eyes you have." The kitten curled up inside the crook of his arm. "You are a clean, well-behaved kitten. I'm sure you are descended from a long line of noble cats."

"She's our cat", one of the boys said suddenly. "Ippolito's and mine. Here, give her to me."

Philip turned around and faced a defiant young boy. He placed the kitten in the boy's outstretched hands without a word.

The older boy, conscious of his brother's impolite manner, said, "You see, Cosma—she's our nurse—

forgot to close the kitchen door and Felicity—that's the kitten's name—crept out. Michele didn't really think you were *stealing* her. Did you, Michele?"

The younger boy shook his head vigorously. "Of course not."

Then Philip said, "She's the most beautiful cat in all Rome."

"We think so, too", Michele said. "Would you like to see Perpetua? She's Felicity's mother."

"I would, very much," said Philip, "but I am waiting to see Messer Galeotto del Caccia.

The boys' eyes widened. "He's our father", they said in unison. Then Ippolito said, "Do you seek alms? Father gives alms on holidays to all who come to his door."

Philip followed the two young del Caccias into the great house, where they left him in an anteroom and ran to fetch their father. Messer Galeotto greeted him kindly, saying that he had once met Philip's father, Ser Francesco, at a meeting of the Great Council. The director general of Customs then asked him for news of Florence. Philip told him what he knew, mentioning in passing that Messer Clemente, the schoolmaster, was now lecturing at the university.

At the mention of Clemente's name, Ser Galeotto's eyes brightened. "You were his pupil?" he asked.

Philip responded enthusiastically that he thought

Ser Clemente a wonderful teacher. He praised his learning and charm at such length and so shrewdly that Galeotto was prompted to say, "Then you are something of a scholar yourself? I wonder now whether you could be a tutor as well as a hermit."

"I do not know what you mean, sir." Philip was puzzled.

"I mean just this. My two boys, Michele and Ippolito, are not happy with their schoolmaster. I think they would be happy with you. Would you consider teaching them a few hours a day? In return I could offer you a room in this house, a florin a month, and your means. What do you say to that?"

Philip paused. Two opposite wishes played tug of war within him. His first desire was to be a hermit. That meant a life of poverty, of fasting, and of prayer. On the other hand he loved children and had been much taken with Michele and Ippolito. Besides, it was a great grace to live in a good Christian home. Could he be both a hermit and a tutor? He begged the Holy Spirit to guide him.

"Messer Galeotto," he said finally, "I will accept your offer provided you will allow me to live as a hermit."

"All I ask," Messer Galeotto replied, "is that you teach my boys two or three hours a day to be Christians and scholars. Beyond that, you are free. Live, eat, sleep where you will. If the arrangements are not satisfactory, we will change them."

Ser Galeotto clapped his hands and a little maid darted into the room. "Bring my sons here", he said.

In a few seconds the two boys were standing before their father and Philip, looking much shier than they had before.

"Boys," Messer Galeotto said, "Messer Filippo de Neri of Florence will teach you from now on. I want you to obey him. No nonsense now, or else! Show Messer Filippo to his room. Introduce him to Cosma and the other servants."

Philip was delighted with his room. It was as bare as he could wish. There was an old bed half-hidden in a corner, a table and a chair, a clothesline, and a wash bucket. A large window slanted from the floor to the ceiling so that he could look out at the blue sky and friendly stars.

Michele and Ippolito stood in respectful silence. They watched Philip warily now since he was no longer a mere stranger but a tutor. Philip pretended to put on a stern look.

"Well," he said, "let's get to our first lesson."

The boys gasped. "A lesson! On a feast day? On Christmas?" Ippolito protested.

"But we haven't got our slates," moaned Michele.

"Our first lesson," insisted Philip, "consists of a riddle. Now listen carefully. If your answer is right, I shall take you for a walk this afternoon.

A cat ate a spider.
It tickled inside her.
Then she drank cider
To stop the tickling inside her.
The poor little spider
Drowned in the cider.
Whatever made the cat eat the poor little spider?

"Oh, I know that one", Ippolito said confidently.

The cat ate the spider
'Cause she couldn't abide her.

"No," cried Michele. "I know a better one."

The cat ate the spider
The better to hide her.

"Both of you arc right," Philip said. "I shall take you for a walk this afternoon."

"I say," Ippolito interrupted, his brown eyes sparkling with the expectation of good days ahead, "you're not half bad as a teacher. Where did you hear about the cat and the spider?"

"Oh," said Philip, "the boys in Florence knew that years ago. That's the way we learned our lessons. Did you ever hear of the fight between the flea and the ant? See if you can tell me who really started the fight.

Said a flea to an ant, "In *our* family tree
We have an aunt who is also a flea."
Said the ant to the flea, "There *can't* be an
ant
In a flea's family tree; 'tis *silly,* you see."
Said the flea to the ant, "An aunt's not an
ant."
"Quite true", said the ant. "Yet you will agree
That ants have aunts who *are* ants in *their* family
tree."
"Agreed", said the flea. "Now *you* will agree
That an aunt's not an ant when she's an aunt of a
flea."
"I'd rather", the ant said, "a million times be
The aunt of an ant than the aunt of a flea."
Then they both agreed that they must disagree,
So the flea bit the ant and the ant bit the flea.

The boys liked this kind of lesson. They laughed and shouted and begged Philip to tell them more stories.

"No more now," he said. "There will be days and days for such lessons. But I will teach you to sing a song for Christmas day. Come, Michele, you sit on my knee. Ippolito, you're as big as I am; you sit on the bed. Now here's the way the song goes." Philip practiced the scales for a moment. When he began to sing, the two boys were hanging on his words:

On Christmas Day in Bethlehem,
The angels to the shepherds sing
Noel, Noel, the Christ is born,
Come, faithful hearts, to heaven's King.

The Father's, Son's, and Spirit's love
For your hearts' loves doth reach and yearn;
Come to the cave, there bring your love
Since love for love is love's return.

They learned the song quickly and sang it over and over again. As they did, the joy of Christmas deepened in their souls. They did not want to leave Philip, even for dinner. When they had to leave, Michele said, "Oh, Messer Filippo, I'm so glad you came to us. I'm so *very* glad."

"And I, too", said Philip, thinking how sweet a task it would be to help these innocent souls know and love their loving Master.

8

THE GLOBE OF FIRE

As the years passed, Philip was supremely happy in Rome. He loved his quiet attic room, his two pupils, his daily walk along the streets of Rome where he talked about God to whoever would listen. Prayer now was such a habit that he could not stop praying, not even when he made up jokes to tease the loafers on the street to get them to confession.

He loved San Girolamo and his work with the confraternity. One of his great joys was to go begging for food and clothing and medicine for the pilgrims and the poor with Persiano Rosa, who was now a priest.

Then there were so many churches to visit—the Dominican Church of the Minerva, where he went often to Mass and to pray the Divine Office; the Church of San Dorotea, where he could sit with the children for hours and play games with them and teach them their catechism. Besides, there were the universities where he could listen to lectures of philosophers and theologians the better to know how to spread God's word among the people of Rome.

But, while Philip spent all his time doing good, he was not blind to the evils of Rome. The sight of worldly priests dressed like courtiers; of bankers fattening on the papal treasury; of stony-hearted nobles building magnificent palaces while the poor starved—all this filled him with anguish. Most of all he detested the Roman carnival, especially the one that was beginning now—the carnival before Lent.

Today Philip planned to go to the Hospital of San Giacomo and then in the cool of the evening to walk out to San Sebastiano just outside the city. He shrank from the thought of spending the carnival night in Rome.

The Via Giulia was an orgy of excitement. It was as if the pagan god Pan had come alive again. A horse-drawn float with actors and actresses impersonating Venus and Adonis was passing by. Behind it great, grimacing, cardboard animals, giants, and clowns bounced crazily up and down and from side to side. Masked musicians played in a frenzy. Violins scraped, horns tooted, drums pounded until Philip's ears ached. Worst of all were the wine-mad shrieks of the crowds. The Romans, by donning their carnival disguises, seemed to cast off their Christianity, even their humanity. They pranced around like wild animals, dancing grotesquely, gesturing crazily.

Philip covered his eyes with his hands. This was evil, evil, evil. Yet it would become worse. As the carnival continued, and wine fired the hot Roman blood, anger and jealousy would hold sway. Men would be throttled in the midst of a blasphemy and sent to death and hell in an instant. And what scandal the carnival gave to the young! How could they ever grow up to know the true meaning of Christianity if they saw, year after year, this animal violence of their elders—yes, even of their parents—in the very heart of Christendom? Philip vowed that he would some day put an end to the carnival—how he did not yet know—but the Lord would counsel him.

At length Philip fought his way through the swarming street. He must get to the Hospital of the Incurables. Today, he knew, the sick would need him more than ever. As in all hospitals at this time there were no regular doctors or nurses. The sick depended on the generosity of volunteers. And today—the height of the carnival—only a few volunteers would venture forth. In his mind's eye he could see the dying old captain he had attended yesterday moaning for water. He redoubled his pace.

On his way he passed the Church of Santa Maria de Monserrato. Could he not spare just one minute for a visit? He pushed aside the leather curtain at the entrance and found, to his great joy, that the church was filled. At the height of the carnival, too!

In the pulpit he saw a small, wiry man whom he recognized immediately as his dear friend, Ignatius of Loyola. The little Basque priest was speaking about the vanity of this world. His Spanish accent made his speech almost unintelligible, but, somehow, the accent and the foreign phrases carried his message. In fact, he hardly needed words to say what he meant. His eyes flamed with love, his gestures clutched at the heart.

Philip stood for a moment entranced. He could see a white light shining over Ignatius' head. Inwardly he said, "The Holy Spirit is in this man." It filled him with great joy to hear Ignatius challenge the vanity of the carnival. Christ had his champions!

Out in the streets the noise was still earsplitting. Philip threaded his way through reeling merrymakers. A girl tried to throw her arms around him. Roughly he shoved her aside. She screamed at him drunkenly. A red-faced youth thrust a flask in his face crying, "Drink, drink, for tomorrow Lent begins." Philip dodged him and continued on.

At the hospital there was another kind of noise. Inside the men's dormitory there was the terrifying discord of pain—low moans, sudden sharp yelps, long, quavering screams, trembling whines. Would to God, Philip prayed, that the merrymakers could listen to this sad music. It would remind them of the vanity of pleasure and sin. He hastened to the bed of the old captain. Bending over him, he put his hand on his shoulder.

"How are you, today, Tommaso?" he asked gently. "Is the wound a little better?"

The old man's eyelids flickered. His withered hand groped for Philip's. "It will not be long now, Philip", he said slowly and closed his eyes.

Philip got a bucket of water and some rags and bandages. Gently he bathed Tommaso's face and hands. He removed the old bandage, cleaned the festering wound on Tommaso's breast, and bandaged it again. Then he swept the floor and brought fresh straw for the mattress. He combed Tommaso's hair and beard. Then he talked to the old man in a gentle voice, telling him how much God admired good soldiers, especially those who suffered for his sake and fought faithfully to the end. That very morning, Philip said, he had seen a picture of Saint Michael, the Archangel, patron of warriors. He knew that Saint Michael would be waiting next to Saint Peter to welcome Tommaso, who had fought so well.

When Tommaso fell asleep Philip crept away quietly to the farther end of the room.

"Ah, my own Marcantonio," he said to a boy of sixteen with bright, feverish eyes, "have you had any food? Let me run down to the kitchen and bring you some soup."

The boy shook his head.

"A drink of water, then? Come drink this."

Marcantonio had a taut, frightened look. Philip held the boy's hot, dry hand. He had run away from home to make his fortune in Rome. Within a month he was down with the black fever. And now he was surely dying, without one of his friends near him. Worse still, Philip feared the boy was tortured by an unconfessed sin. Once more he begged him, "Just say the word and I will bring a priest to you, Marcantonio. It is so simple, so easy to confess your sins. Your soul will be at rest then."

Marcantonio shook his head. Tears welled in his eyes. He hid his face with his arms.

"No! No! God would never forgive me for cheating him and lying to him all these years. He couldn't. I belong in hell."

"Do not say such a thing! It is Satan who told you to say that. Listen, Marcantonio, listen."

Philip sat by the boy's bed and held his head in

his arms. "Do you not know that I would forgive you now if you had lied to me and cheated me? Look into my eyes and tell me—would I not forgive you?"

Marcantonio's eyes softened as he gazed at Philip. "Well, would I forgive you? Tell me."

"Oh, Filippo," Marcantonio sobbed, "I feel that you see through me and know all that I have ever done. It pains me to think of my past. Yes, yes, *you* would forgive me."

"Well, then," said Philip, praying intensely to the Holy Spirit, "is your Father in heaven less forgiving than I am? Come, Marcantonio. Do but ask him in your heart for his forgiveness."

Philip held up the crucifix he wore on a chain around his neck.

"Look at Jesus. He died for you. He is praying for you now. He is saying, 'Father, forgive him.' He waits only for you to pray with him."

Marcantonio moaned.

"Listen," Philip said, "I will say the Act of Contrition out loud and you say it to yourself. Perhaps it will be easier that way."

Then he recited the Act of Contrition aloud. Halfway through he noticed Marcantonio's lips beginning to move. "I—firmly—resolve—with the help—of thy grace—to confess my sins . . ."

"Oh, my Marcantonio, you have said it."

Philip gently released the boy's head and slipped

from his side. Never had he run so quickly. He almost bumped into the litter bearers at the end of the corridor. Where was a priest? Where? He heard a bell tinkling upstairs in the women's dormitory.

Upstairs he flew, two steps at a time, begging Marcantonio's guardian angel to make sure that it was the Eucharistic bell that was ringing. Thanks be to God it was a priest, none other than Messer Francesco Xavier, Ignatius' companion. He was bringing Communion to the women.

Philip waited on his knees until Messer Francesco came out of the dormitory. Philip signaled the acolyte, who preceded the priest with candle and bell, to follow him. The three made their way through the crowded rooms to Marcantonio's bed.

When the acolyte placed the candle on the floor, Philip noticed the boy's eyes were closed. For a moment he thought it was too late. But no! As Messer Francesco whispered into Marcantonio's ear, "I have brought our dear Lord Christ to save you", the boy's eyes opened. Quickly Philip placed a screen around the bed and withdrew.

"Father in heaven," he prayed, "he is young. Forgive him. Overwhelm him with your love. May his confession be pure and whole and may he live again in the innocence of his baptism."

Messer Francesco was finished. He was on his feet now, removing his stole. Philip glanced at the little Spanish priest, his whole expression a mute, worried question. Messer Francesco gave him a smile so sweet and radiant that Philip was sure of the answer.

"Do not be anxious, Messer Filippo", he said. "Our friend is at peace. He has confessed and received Communion, the last Host I had. He is sleeping quietly now."

"Thanks be to God!" Philip said fervently. "Praised be his Mercy."

"What other clients do you have for me, Filippo?" the priest asked.

"Ah," said Philip, "my old captain will need you soon to anoint him. And, by God's mercy, Gennaro, the goldsmith, has asked your reverence to visit him."

The priest gazed fondly at Philip. "Messer Filippo," he said, "why do you not become a priest? Our father Ignatius would welcome you into our company. Do you know what he said about you? That you send him more penitents and more novices than any man in Rome. That you are like a bell that calls men to church without itself leaving the bell tower."

Philip laughed. "Ignatius would welcome me because he is a marvel of generosity. But he is an eagle while I am a sparrow."

"Messer Filippo," Francesco said gently, "do not deceive yourself. I tell you with sure knowledge that God expects much of you. More than you think."

Humbly Philip bowed his head. There was a radiance about this man as there was about Ignatius. Every shred of his being glowed with a love of God. To be near him was to know surely that Christ lived on in his church, working and suffering, healing and redeeming, now, as in the days of his life on earth.

"Pray for me, Messer Francesco."

"And you for me, Messer Filippo."

"Always", the priest said.

"I, too," Philip said.

Then Francesco left him, a long, loving question in his eyes, and Philip returned to his visits—to washing, and cleaning, and feeding, and talking to the men in the wards.

When he left the hospital Philip felt distracted and spent. He yearned for the fresh air of the Roman Campagna, the countryside just outside the city walls. Once more he fought his way through the revelers, but this time he was too tired to notice their frivolities.

He reached the Appian Way as dusk set in. Here was the world as God had made it—tranquil, innocent, and beautiful. In the purple twilight the plain spread out like a rich tapestry, dotted here and there with clusters of poplar trees, the brown thatched huts of the peasants, the saffron-colored marble villas of the nobles, the stark white tombs of the ancient Romans. Flocks of sheep moved slowly along crisscrossed paths to their night pastures. Cowbells tinkled and birds sang, and a cool, clean breeze swept down from the hills. Philip breathed in the fragrance of heather and thyme and felt his energies revive. Soon he would reach the Basilica of San Sebastiano and there he would rest.

For all his love of San Sebastiano he could never behold it without a pang. The roof had fallen in and the walls were crusted with moss and shrouded in wild ivy and brambles. The altar, stripped and desolate, lay under a heap of charred stones. The skeleton of a horse protruding from the rubble reminded him that the imperial cavalry had used the church as a stable during the sack of Rome.

Philip went into the deserted church and found a lantern he had left under a stone. He lit it and then, walking carefully, he discovered the opening to the catacombs. The steps led sharply downward. Then the passage veered to the left, then down again through soft, porous rock. Finally he came to a large, square vault. Here, on one of the tombs cut into the side of the catacombs, he placed his lantern.

For a long time he rested. The impressions of the carnival and the hospital began to recede. It was as if, having seen visions of hell and of purgatory, he had at last reached the region of the blessed. The bones of martyrs, confessors, virgins, and widows were sleeping here triumphantly awaiting their resurrection. Here were the saints who had lived and suffered and died for Christ and now lived with him in glory.

Stirred by the memory of these early Christians, he began to pray for the conversion of Rome. He called upon all the blessed buried in this vault to beg God's mercy for all Christians, in Rome and throughout the world, for all men in all countries. As he prayed, Philip became more and more aware that Jesus alone was life and all else was death. He kept repeating, "I love thee, Lord, I love thee—yet I do not love thee enough."

He called on the Holy Spirit, the spirit of love, to come into his heart so that he could love Jesus with his own divine love, and, with Jesus, to give thanks to the Father.

"Spirito, Spirito", he murmured over and over again. "Give me thy love that I may love thee, and our Father and his adorable Son. Come Holy Ghost, Creator blest, and in our hearts take up thy rest. Come fill the heart that thou hast made."

He kept on praying. Then, just as it happened before in the grotto at Gaeta, Philip felt his body tremble, and his heart pound, and the blood sing in his ears. He saw a globe of fire—more brilliant than all the suns he had ever seen. It hovered before him. It moved nearer. It was now so close that it seemed to touch him, and he was struck dumb with delight because he felt sure that the fire was the flame of the Holy Spirit.

He struggled now to pray. "Lord, open my mouth that I may praise thy Holy Name."

As his lips opened, the ball of fire entered his mouth. He could feel it pouring into him, down to his very heart. Now Philip was sure that he had never yet loved God before, for so great was the surge of his love for God that his soul almost tore itself free from his body. At the same time his heart was burning with the heat of a thousand fires. He ripped open his cloak and threw himself on the cool damp floor of the vault.

As the heat increased, so too did the pounding of his heart. It was swelling. He placed his hand on his heart. He felt a lump on his breast, growing with every pulsation. It was now as large as his fist. It was divine love that was filling his heart, for he felt no pain but a great joy, a piercing sweetness, an overwhelming confidence. If God gave him any more of his love, Philip felt, his heart would break.

Hours later the fire in his breast and the trembling and the pounding ceased. But his heart remained swollen and his feeling of love for God had not abated. He wanted to stretch out his arms and embrace the whole world and bring all men to Christ.

"Dear Jesus," he prayed with divine impatience, "I have done nothing. When will you let me bring back your lost sheep? Teach me your ways so that men may find me meek and forgiving and merciful and wise—so that they won't see me at all, but only you. Let Philip cease to exist, save to be your mouth and hands and eyes and heart."

9

PHILIP BECOMES A PRIEST

PHILIP ALWAYS FELT he was not worthy to be a priest, although through the years he had prepared many others for the priesthood. Both Michele and Ippolito, his former pupils, were priests now and so, too, were many of his early friends in Rome.

But Philip thought the priesthood was too great an honor for him. As he said to Persiano Rosa, when his old friend and confessor brought up the matter for perhaps the thousandth time, "God needs little servants as well as big ones. I am by nature a little servant. I am good for running errands and managing the affairs of the confraternity."

Yet Persiano's persistence was gradually making Philip change his mind. "Ah, but Philip," Persiano would say, "look about you. People still go to confession and Communion only once a year. As a layman what can you do about that? Nothing. They will not listen to you. Frequent reception of the sacraments is for hermits, they say, and they excuse themselves. But as a priest you could advise them in the confessional, as I do, that they should go once a month or oftener. In that way you could come closer to your heart's desire—that all Rome come closer to Christ."

Yes, Persiano's arguments were strong. Philip knew well that the priesthood was a higher state of life, and that, as a priest, he could help more souls. Yet he hesitated. He still clung to the humble freedom of a hermit's life, but he never ceased praying for the grace to do God's will.

One day, standing in the garden of San Girolamo, Philip was imploring the Holy Spirit to guide him to a right choice. As it happened so often now when he prayed to the Holy Spirit, he felt his heart pound and a fire of love steal through him.

"Dear God, Most Holy Trinity," he begged, "this love of yours will slay me. It is too much. I cannot bear much more. If your love fills me so much now, what would it do if I were to hold you in my hands?"

In his joy he began to sing. Then he heard the

gate rasp on its hinges. A tall, bent figure, wrapped in a coarse hermit's cloak, moved like a spent shadow along the wall of the church. As the man passed, Philip caught a glimpse of his dark, pitted face, his cancerous mouth. The man's eyes were riveted on the ground, but, as he passed Philip, he shot a glance at him and then stopped suddenly.

"Are you not Philip Neri?" the man said. "Messer Rosa told me about you. I am Buonsignore Cacciaguerra."

Philip bowed. He tried not to look at Cacciaguerra's ruined face.

"I have seen your reverence many times since you have come to live at San Girolamo."

Cacciaguerra's burning eyes seemed to probe into his own questioningly. Philip blushed. "Perhaps you were wondering why I was singing. It is because I . . ."

Cacciaguerra interrupted him. "You need not tell me", he said. "There are moments when the heart is too full, too full."

"There are, there are," Philip said.

He longed to tell this priest, already renowned for his holiness, of his struggle to decide between the vocations of a hermit and of a priest.

Cacciaguerra kept staring at Philip, as if reading his thoughts. Finally, Philip said, "Messer Cacciaguerra, will you help me?"

Then he told the priest of Persiano Rosa's suggestion, of his doubts, and of his conviction of his own unworthiness.

The priest paused. Then he said, "If you become a priest, Philip, you will find out many things. We are all unworthy of the priesthood, unworthy of being second Christs. But the greatest unworthiness is to make our unworthiness an excuse to be more unworthy. There are priests in Rome who say Mass only once a month. They say they are unworthy to say Mass more often. I say to them, 'Make yourselves worthy.' And how can we make ourselves worthy? First by staying in the state of grace; then by saying Mass daily, by receiving Christ daily."

The priest spoke so intensely that his thin frame quivered. He paused and bit his underlip. Suddenly, he said, "You have a moment?"

"All day", Philip replied.

"Come then", Cacciaguerra said, leading him to the bench near the wall. When they were seated the priest folded his hands in the sleeves of his cloak. Fixing his eyes on his feet and rocking to and fro, as if in pain, he said, "I tell you this story because it may help you make your decision. It may help you to realize what great good comes from the Mass and from daily Communion, what great good a priest can do for himself and for others."

"Once there was a young merchant from Siena

who went to Palermo, in Sicily, to make his fortune. The Lord gave him a handsome frame, a good wit, a power of friendship. All of these he abused. He wasted his body in his lust for an evil woman, his wit in the amassing of gold, his friendship on wastrels. He grew richer and richer. His ships brought back treasures from the east and the west.

"All this he used for his pleasure—feasts, slaves, garments of gold cloth. He would wear a garment oncc and destroy it, the better to proclaim his wealth and magnificence.

"But his faith was not wholly dead. Once a year he went to confession and Communion. For two days or so he repented of his crimes. Then he would fall back to his lusts, his avarice, his luxuries."

Buonsignore Cacciaguerra shuddered as if the tale were too horrible to repeat. As Philip listened, he thought of the prodigal son who had wasted his substance and was forgiven, and then of the magnificent young men of Rome—princes, courtiers, and artists—who were not unlike the rich merchant of Palermo, not unlike the prodigal son. He, too, was saddened.

"The young merchant", Cacciaguerra continued, "rose and fell on the tides of passion. Finally one year—just as he had performed his Easter duty—the merchant was walking home alone. He heard a groan. He turned and saw Jesus himself, a cord around his neck, carrying his Cross. 'My son,'

Christ said brokenheartedly, 'see how thou art treating me. I beg of thee, do not drive me from thee.' Later the apparition appeared again.

"Remorse ate at the young man's heart. Misfortunes began to afflict him. His ships foundered. An enemy slashed his face with a dagger. Pirates captured him. In the marketplace near Palermo a possessed woman screamed out his sins for all to hear. His soul was in torment.

"But when he tried to reform himself, his brothers and friends laughed at him. Vowing himself to poverty, he crawled about Italy and Spain, a pilgrim, a penitent. In the holy city of Saint James, at Compostela, he begged for pardon. Home again in Palermo, wretched, eaten by disease, cast off by all save an old Negress who had been one of his slaves, the merchant was purified by his afflictions.

"Then, by Christ's mercy, the merchant was inspired to receive Communion every day. This most wretched man, this castoff, was restored to grace. He became a hermit. He preached in Rome, in Milan, in Abruzzi, Naples, Nola, Barcelona. By God's grace his preaching turned men from their evil ways. Finally, he yielded to the wishes of his superiors—and became a priest.

"All this, my good Philip, is God's mercy shown through the Sacrament of his Body and Blood. By the Sacrament the merchant turned from sin.

By the Sacrament he learned God's love. Now he lives by the Sacrament and yearns only to spread its devotion."

Buonsignore Cacciaguerra rose from the bench. He turned his ravaged face towards Philip.

"I was that merchant. Learn well from me that he who was once in sin can now be consoled by the blessed spirit of God—the blessed spirit that can, in a flash, transform the soul and fill it with such immeasurable delights, can melt it with such delights that the soul forgets its carnal nature. Oh, Philip, in your priesthood be to sinners as Christ is to me—forgiving, loving beyond all comprehension. Draw them back, draw them ever to the Most Holy Sacrament of the Eucharist. I have no more to say. I shall pray for you. You pray for me."

The priest blessed Philip and went into the house. Philip was shaken by the story of Buonsignore Cacciaguerra. He felt chastened, grave, yet confident. God could change men's hearts as he had Cacciaguerra's. There was hope then for Rome and for the whole world. He looked up at the sky. The white sun shone like a Host lifted up in sacrifice.

"Oh my dear, dear Lord—dear, dear, dear Lord. If you accept me as your priest, grant me the favor of your love for souls. Give me your great love for sinners so that this love of yours will pour through me upon the heads and into the hearts of sinners."

Philip stood still in the garden, listening to the

voice of God speaking within him. He hardly knew that time was passing.

Finally, when his trembling ceased, he went upstairs to the little cell where he knew Persiano Rosa would be waiting. He knocked at the door.

"Come in, come in", Persiano called out in his warm, happy voice. "Ah, Philip, it is you. What good are you up to?"

"Persiano," Philip said, "it is finished. I have decided. It is God's will that I become a priest."

Persiano Rosa jumped with joy. He embraced Philip heartily, tears of joy streaming down his face. When he regained his composure, he said, "I will myself prepare you for the priesthood, Filippo. We must begin at once. Here, take this book of Saint Thomas home with you. Come back tomorrow. In the meantime I will go at once to my dear friend Giovanni Lunelli, the bishop of Sebaste, to recommend that he accept you for ordination after your studies. I must see, too, whether the confraternity will allow you to live in the spare room down the hall. Oh, Philip, think of it, you may be one of us at San Girolamo after all!"

All these possibilities stunned Philip. "Did you feel as terrified as I do when you decided to be a priest?" Philip asked his friend.

"Terrified? I was as if stricken dumb. Your own babbling Persiano was stunned into silence. But isn't that as it should be?"

"Yes", said Philip quietly.

From that point on Philip withdrew from all activities save that of preparation for the priesthood.

As each day began now Philip's first thought was of his coming ordination. He would wake up, as was his habit, with the Holy Name upon his lips, and a new holy fear in his heart. He was almost relieved that this was not yet the day of Holy Orders! The closer he came to ordination the more unworthy he felt. With his confessor's permission, for daily Communion was rare in those days, he received the Sacrament each morning. Then, for a long time afterwards, he would beg God's help in the path he was about to take.

"My Jesus, if thou uphold me not, I shall fall. My Jesus, what shall I do if thou dost not help me? My Jesus, if thou dost not help me, I am ruined. Virgin Mary, Mother of God, pray to Jesus for me. My Jesus, if thou would have me, clear away all the hindrances which keep me from thee."

Afterwards he studied—in the library at San Girolamo, in Persiano's cell, in his attic room at the house of the del Caccias, wherever he could best find quiet. When he came upon a difficult passage he marked it carefully. He could ask Persiano or Buonsignore Cacciaguerra. Or he could consult the Dominicans, Capuchins, Jesuits. He had the pick of the scholars of Rome.

But as the day came closer he studied less than he prayed; rather his prayers and his studies intermingled. His confidence grew, not because he trusted himself, but because he knew and felt that God would provide him with all the graces he needed. "Let me not get in the way of your graces, God."

The day came for the subdiaconate. Thanks be to God he had a few weeks more to prepare for the diaconate. And when that ceremony was over, he would have almost a month to prepare for the priesthood itself. Philip was grateful for this gradual approach to the altar. Each step strengthened him for the next one. It might have been too great a strain suddenly to be lifted, as if on a cloud, to the mount of God. The ascent was best taken gradually, as the Church, in her motherly wisdom, decreed.

Finally the day of ordination itself came. On the twenty-third of May, 1551, at the Church of San Tommaso in Parime, Bishop Lunelli consecrated Philip a priest. It was for Philip a day of surpassing joy. He was Christ's beloved and Christ was his beloved Lord—forever. His heart burned with an almost unbearable fire, melted in a sweetness he could not describe, because now he realized it could continue and increase and grow more intense forever and ever.

He was thirty-six years old the day he became a priest. It seemed to him that he had reached the full flower of his life. What else could be added?

The weeks that followed his ordination were full of inexpressible joy. Philip was barely conscious of the glorious Roman spring. Rather it was the springtime of his priesthood, of his new friendship with Christ that Philip savored with all humility and gratitude.

To be a priest was to be another Christ. That meant to think Christ's thoughts, to feel as he felt, to do his Father's will, to live always according to his Holy Spirit. So Philip tried to live.

He was not even aware of his own fervor. But his friends at San Girolamo—Persiano Rosa and Buonsignore Cacciaguerra—could have told him that he was living in Christ and Christ was living in him. Philip said Mass every day with extraordinary devotion. The sobs that shook his small frame as he consecrated the bread and the wine moved his congregation to tears. They began to understand how truly the Mass was a reenactment of Calvary. Philip was so absorbed in the sacrifice of the Mass that his server often had to pull on his vestments and whisper, even shout, "Father Philip, you have read the gospel. It is now ten minutes since you have read the gospel."

During the elevation of the Host, Philip, trembling all over, seemed to be raised up above the predella, as if drawn toward his eucharistic King. When he drank from the chalice his teeth clung to the cup.

This embarrassed him, but he could not stop. He employed every device to keep himself from displaying his tremendous fervor. He tapped his feet. He even jingled the key to his room. He instructed his servers to interrupt him. Rather than shock the less fervent members of the congregation, he arranged to say the last Mass when few could observe him. Later he would receive permission to say his Mass privately. Then, after serving the water and wine, the acolyte would lock the door of the chapel and Philip would, for hours, be alone with his adorable Master, exchanging wordlessly the gift of heart for Heart.

The Mass was the greatest event in Philip's every day—its very soul, the power behind all his work and prayer. He came from it renewed and inspired. After Mass his server brought him his main meal—two little loaves of bread and a flask of wine. No more. Later he would not even take the winc. If anyone sent more food he gave it away, either to the ever hungry young altar boys or to a beggar.

After dinner Philip read his breviary in the cloister. He marvelled that the psalms and prayers, the hymns and canticles of his breviary chimed and echoed the Sacrifice of the Mass. Especially in those early weeks of the priesthood, reciting his office brought him a new sense of the communion of saints. As a layman he knew that all Christians were members of Christ's body, branches of a single vine. But how much more he realized this as he recited the Divine Office. Now his voice uttered words of praise to God in union with all God's priests throughout the ages. Together they thanked God, they blessed him and begged for his mercy. Truly the Office—the official prayer of the Church—was prayer such as our Lord himself must now be offering for all his brothers and sisters before the throne of his father in heaven.

Now, brimming with God's love, Philip returned to the church. He sat in the confessional, waiting. He humbly reminded himself, "Now I am in Christ's place."

He kept before him Christ's love of the sinner—of the Samaritan woman whom he pardoned at the well; of Mary Magdalen, whom he raised to be a saint; of the penitent thief; the denying Peter; of all the men and women for whom he suffered and prayed, "Father, forgive them, for they know not what they do."

"I beg thee, most merciful Father," Philip whispered, "send me thy prodigal sons, thy lost sheep. Give me too the grace not only to dispense thy mercy, but to be merciful as thou art merciful."

He fingered his rosary, begging our Lady, as the Refuge of Sinners, to lead her wounded children to this narrow confessional that was so truly a place of healing, a gate to heaven.

He did not have to wait long. Soon they began

to come to him. They came that day, and the next, and the next, and the next. Soon Philip spent most of his days in the confessional. Penitents came to him in the mornings and at night, men and women of all classes—princes and beggars, priests and cardinals. He had a special gift for speaking directly to each individual soul, for saying the exact words that helped each man to be sorry for his particular sins and faults and to live closer to Christ.

To a boy who worried needlessly, he said, "Go in peace, my son. God will be with you in all your temptations. You have but to call on him."

"My daughter," he counseled a woman, "you have the feeling that you will go to hell. Nonsense. For whom did Christ die? For sinners, you say? Then, since you are a sinner, he died for you. Your fear is a temptation."

"Go ahead," he whispered to a penitent musician overcome with remorse, "weep. You may weep on my heart if you choose. God understands you are sorry. Have you never wept on your own father's breast? You have? Well, then God is your Father, too. He understands you better than you do yourself. Weep. But after you weep you must remember to laugh, too. Laugh because God has forgiven you. Laugh for joy. I give you a penance. You must stand on the Corso and laugh for one whole minute. If anyone asks you why, say you are a good Christian."

A young man told him he wanted to become a priest. Philip said to him, "You have a vocation? How do you know? Ah, yes, you feel drawn to the sacraments. That is good. But you also feel drawn to your work in the bank. You wish to become rich. A vocation and riches do not go together. It is not riches that will save the world. Give up your avarice and I will believe you have a vocation. In the meantime, I ask you to give alms. Go—today—to the Hospital of San Giovanni. Empty your purse among the sick poor. Then, come again to confession. Come every day if need be."

Another young man feared bad companions. "That fear is a holy fear", Philip told him. "Your guardian angel has placed it there. Why cannot you avoid them? You have no one else to talk to? Well, if you wish, come to my room in the afternoon. We shall sing a little together."

No wonder they kept coming to him, not only to confession, but to his room afterwards. There was hardly room for them in Philip's cell, but they sat on the floor, the bed, the window seat and laughed at his jokes.

He held them entranced by his gossip about the saints, by his vivid descriptions of the joys of heaven. By his playfulness, too, for he was not above boxing their ears or dousing them with a jug of water. Sometimes, too, he read from the

Lives of the Saints, or from Cassian's *Conferences,* but never at length. He stopped at some passage—on humility, for instance, his favorite virtue. He showed them how to practice humility in their everyday lives.

"Take Enrico, for instance. He is very vain about his fine velvet doublet."

Enrico, an ardent admirer of Philip, declared, "I shall never wear it again."

"Nonsense", Philip said. "You must wear decent clothes in your way of life. But you must not be proud of your appearance. Just remember," he said, "all that we are is God's creation, all that we have is God's gift, as the good we do is God's inspiration. What is left is ourselves—that is, nothing. We are nothing except what God has made and given to us."

Sometimes, on holy days, when the young men were free from work, Philip would take them to his favorite churches. They would return late in the evening for prayers at San Girolamo, or at the Minerva where they joined the Dominicans in chanting the Office. Thus Philip kept his young men under his eye—reining them in gently, leading, not forcing, them to a more perfect life. His zeal was bearing fruit. San Girolamo became the center of spiritual life in Rome. Hundreds came daily to pray, to listen to sermons, above all to go to confession and Communion.

Philip, together with Persiano Rosa and Buonsignore Cacciaguerra, drove himself to the point of exhaustion in his priestly tasks. But he was gloriously happy. What more joy could anyone imagine than this joy of bringing men to Christ and Christ to men? Indeed, he was so wholly absorbed in his work that he did not see the first sign of the fire of suspicion and misunderstanding that would soon become a scorching blaze of undeserved contempt.

10

TRIED BY FIRE

SOME OF THE PRIESTS at San Girolamo were chaplains of the Confraternity of Charity; some, like Buonsignore Cacciaguerra and Philip, merely lived there as guests. Since Philip had no official connection with the confraternity he never interfered in its activity, save to hear the confessions of the members or to celebrate Mass for their intentions. But he loved the work of the confraternity and felt he was part of it. Hence he could not at first understand the animosity of one of its most important officials, Vincenzo Teccosi.

Teccosi, a physician from Fabriano, was one of

the four deputies of the confraternity appointed to take care of the business activities of San Girolamo. It was he who regularly visited the chaplains, paid their stipends, arranged for services, furnished sacristans, acolytes, sextons, and saw to it that the church was kept clean and well decorated. A good man, Teccosi was devoted to the poor. His neighbors admired his charity, his competence, his judgment.

But, like other good men, he was a little too sure of himself. When he did not like something, instead of saying he did not *like* it, he was inclined to say it was *wicked*.

One thing he did not like was the activity of Buonsignore Cacciaguerra. The priest annoyed him. As a physician he saw clearly that the priest was a sick man—cancerous, ill-nourished, exhausted. He also thought quite honestly that he was sick in soul.

"I tell you," Vincenzo said to one of the other deputies, "this Cacciaguerra will give San Girolamo a bad name. Do you know what he is doing? He is making a women's club out of the place. Every time I go near the church what do I see? Madonna Paola, or Madonna Faustina, or Felice da Barbarano—visionaries all of them—and many others listening to his conferences on meditation and union with God. He is as mad as the Jesuits with all their nonsense about thirty-day retreats. Women should be home minding their houses. He has them living like nuns. I tell you, he's mad."

His friend, Jacopo, said that Cacciaguerra would bear watching.

"And the new priest, Philip Neri, too. Upon my word, he has the place cluttered up with youngsters day and night."

Jacopo lowered his voice to a whisper.

"What's more—and this I don't like at all—this Philip, and Cacciaguerra, too, are very, very imprudent. Last Thursday—Thursday, mind you, a weekday—I dropped into church. What did I see? Rows upon rows of people going to Communion! Who were they? Married women, children, even workmen. All people of the world; not a religious among them. If this keeps up there will be no distinction between religious and seculars. A priest I know said it strikes a blow at vocations. He said that he heard this Philip actually proposes to make people 'religious worldlings'. What nonsense!"

Teccosi shook his head in disgust.

"You are right. This Philip is well-meaning but a dangerous visionary. Birds of a feather flock together. He is hand and glove with Cacciaguerra."

Suspicion is vigilant. The suspicious deputies decided to talk things over with the chaplains—all except Persiano Rosa.

"We don't want to start trouble, reverend fathers, but we do want you to know how we feel", Teccosi said to the three chaplains behind the closed door of the library of San Girolamo.

"This is our church, that is, the confraternity's", he went on. "The cardinal protector has given *us* charge of it and *you* are our chaplains. In recent months one would not think we had anything to do with San Girolamo. It is known as Philip Neri's church and as Cacciaguerra's church."

Ser Vincenzo grew excited as he talked.

"Only yesterday my friend Anerio told me that his wife Fulvia went to confession here. Philip Neri told her to go make beds at the orphanage at the Piazza Capronica. A woman of Fulvia's position! She went and brought back bedbugs. I gave Anerio a piece of my mind. 'Are you a man or a doormat?' I said. 'Tell her to keep away from this Florentine midget. Send her to a good, old-fashioned priest who'll tell her what a woman's place really is.' "

Jacopo and the three chaplains nodded their heads in agreement. One of the chaplains, a pale, serious man, said, "But what can we do, Ser Vincenzo? There is no superior in this house. Ser Buonsignore can do as he pleases, as can Ser Filippo. Only yesterday, I understand, Ser Buonsignore went to our cardinal protector and requested him to *reform* our house. He demanded that all priests say Mass and hear confessions every day, or whenever they are requested to do so, and that they refuse stipends for Masses and for administering the sacraments.

And he is not even a chaplain of the confraternity."

Ser Vincenzo was incensed. "What? He went to the cardinal? We'll see about that. It seems to me that we had better reform *them*."

He paced about the room and pounded his palms together. "I'll take this matter up with the cardinal protector myself. If I get no satisfaction from him, I'll go to the cardinal vicar of Rome. If necessary I'll go to the Pope himself. What audacity! What presumption when mere guests in our monastery act as if they owned it! They have gone too far. We cannot tolerate such abuses at San Girolamo." It was a stormy meeting.

The doctor was a man of his word. He brought up the abuses, as he called them, at the next meeting of the confraternity. He hinted at the dangers of fanaticism and emotional claptrap. As soon as he opened the subject, others spoke.

A man who prided himself on his scholarship questioned Cacciaguerra's theological knowledge. A man who had witnessed Philip's trembling said that he felt the floor shake and wondered whether perhaps the little priest was possessed by evil spirits. Another argued that both Cacciaguerra and Philip encouraged laymen—worse still, laywomen—to enjoy the spiritual privileges reserved to monks and nuns, namely, meditation, fasting, and frequent reception of the sacraments.

At the end of the meeting it was agreed that

they should ask the cardinal protector to dismiss Philip and Cacciaguerra, or, at least, to curb their activities.

This decision pleased Ser Vincenzo very much. The authorities in Rome did not like newfangled devotions. He was sure they would, at very least, rebuke these upstart priests.

But they didn't. Suspicious as they were of heresy, the authorities found no harm in either of the two priests. Rather they saw that here were true reformers. Philip and Cacciaguerra were leading men back to the Church, back to Christ. A Jesuit theologian, a Dominican theologian, and a Capuchin theologian agreed that it was wise to encourage those who were free from grave sin and desired a more perfect life to confess and receive Communion frequently.

They advised the cardinal protector to reject Teccosi's request. They said emphatically that Philip and Cacciaguerra were simply bringing back the customs of the early Church, of the times when Christians lived and died for the Faith.

Ser Vincenzo should have been content with these decisions. Actually, of course, they infuriated him. "Is there any wonder that heresy has made such headway in Italy and Europe? Pretty soon we shall see Rome overrun by fools."

The poor man was so blinded by his loss of face that, instead of worrying about his patients, or about the conspiracies of the Roman princes, he worried about the priests at San Girolamo. Instead of being concerned about the murders, poisonings, cheatings, and faithlessness that stained Roman society, or even about the threat of another invasion of the papal states, he convinced himself that Cacciaguerra and Philip were imposters and frauds.

Then he stooped to a madly malicious act. Among his many acquaintances Ser Vincenzo numbered two runaway monks. Almost without self-respect, they drifted about Rome, spying and doing odd jobs along the waterfront. When Teccosi cast about for someone to help him carry out his plan, he thought of them. Yet even they shrank from doing what he proposed. When Ser Vincenzo mentioned that he wanted to appoint them as sacristans at San Girolamo, they thought he was mad.

Arminio, the elder one, exclaimed, "A sacristan! Surely, Ser Vincenzo, you are joking? It is the least appropriate job in the world for me. For Leone, too. We are runaway monks."

Leone, short, fat, surly, shrugged his shoulders. "For pay?" he asked. "How much?"

"I will pay you out of my own pocket", the physician said. "Two whole ducats a month for each of you."

Then Ser Vincenzo explained what he wanted them to do. They were to dress the altars, prepare the linens and vestments, take care of the sacristy. This they must surely know how to do. They nodded.

But this was not all. Their real job was to help him get rid of two insolent priests. Had they heard of Cacciaguerra and Philip Neri? They had? Good. They despised them for their whining piety? Good again. So did Ser Vincenzo and many others. So it was agreed? Arminio and Leone would deal with them.

"Make them uncomfortable", Ser Vincenzo said. "Go as far as you like—short of killing them, of course."

Arminio and Leone were quietly installed as sacristans.

At first Philip was hardly aware of these new fellows, as Persiano Rosa called them. They were, he thought, perhaps a little too bustling. They came close to irreverence in handling the altar cards, the candlesticks, the linens. They shouted their instructions to the servers, even when Mass was going on. In their presence he was aware, too, of an unpleasant odor—not the smell of honest sweat but a stench that he had come to associate with the presence of sin.

Then he could not fail to notice that they were ignoring him. One day Philip arrived to vest for Mass. No vestments had been prepared for him.

He waited until Arminio arrived in the sacristy. Courteously he asked if he might have a set of vestments.

Arminio scowled at him. "If you had got here earlier you'd have had vestments."

The sacristan contemptuously scooped up an alb, chasuble, maniple, and cincture that had just been worn by another priest and threw them at Philip. "Crawl into these", he said.

Philip mildly protested that they were too big for him. "Besides," he said, "these are black vestments. Today I have been assigned a votive Mass of the Virgin."

"Go find your own vestments, then", Arminio shouted.

A scandalized little altar boy standing in the corner joined Philip in his search. But the smaller vestments were all hidden. Eventually Philip did wear the large, black vestments.

The next day he had to search for altar wine. The day after, he was on his way to the side altar assigned to him when Leone caught his arm, swung him about roughly, and snarled at him, "You there, get up on the high altar where everyone can see what a fraud you are."

Each day they invented a new persecution. They hid the key to the tabernacle so that Philip could not distribute Communion. They posted a sign warning the laity they could receive Communion only at the five o'clock Mass. When Philip wept during Mass, as he did often, they mocked him ferociously.

Cacciaguerra also felt their mockery and scorn, but they left the other priests alone.

"It is inescapable", Buonsignore said to Philip. "They mean to drive us out. Teccosi has put them up to it. I protested to him the other day and he laughed at me. 'There are other churches in Rome', he said. 'Why not try the chapels in the catacombs? No one would bother you there.' "

Philip wept bitterly. "My dear Cacciaguerra," he said, "It is not the humiliation I mind, although I confess it is bitter to take. But they are profaning God's house. They are driving people away. Even the other priests are beginning to say, 'What is the good of so many confessions and Communions anyway? The old ways were better.' "

The older man comforted him. "Nothing is won without sacrifice", Cacciaguerra said. "And this is the sacrifice Christ demands of us. There are two lives a man can give up to the Christ—the life of the body and the life of his good name. Sometimes it is harder to give up the second life than it is to give up the first. Let us freely offer our happiness and reputation to the good Lord. Let us welcome this suffering. In the end truth will prevail."

It was a daily death, a daily martyrdom. Never once to murmur or complain, never once to yield to a feeling of anger, never once to cry out against the abominable scurrilities that were heaped upon him—this taxed Philip's patience to the utmost.

Once, in the middle of Mass, gazing at the crucifix, Philip cried out in his heart, "O good Jesus, why is it thou dost not hear me? See how long a time I have begged thee to give me patience! Why is it that thou hast not heard me, and why is my soul disquieted with thoughts of anger and impatience?"

In his heart he heard an answer, in a voice at once gentle and firm. "Dost thou ask of me patience, Philip? Behold, I will give it to thee speedily on this condition—that if thou in thy heart desire it, then earn it through these temptations of thine."

Patience, then, was to be earned by enduring trials, by meekness and forgiveness. Henceforth Philip never stood before his tormentors without thinking of Christ before the servants of the Pharisees—Christ, the stainless One, spurned with insults, with blows, with spittle. Was he greater than his Master? Christ prayed for his persecutors. So too did Philip. He even tried, in his gentle way, to convert them.

One day, two years after the persecution had begun, when Arminio seemed less malicious than usual, Philip said, "Brother Arminio, would it not be better for you to go back to your monastery? You are unhappy here. Nor will you ever be happy until you fulfill your promise to God. Then God will reward you. I know in my heart you will soon be reconciled with him."

He had caught the man off balance. Arminio was startled that Philip talked to him after the way he had insulted Philip. The soft, caressing tone of the priest's voice melted Arminio's heart. A scalding pang of remorse blinded his eyes. He felt a need, almost a wish, to fall on his knees, to confess his sins on the spot, and to run as fast as his legs could carry him back to the monastery he had abandoned. It would be so easy.

This Philip, for all the abominable things he had said of him, was a good man, goodness itself. He had seen other clerics, worldly men dressed in velvet gowns, bedecked with golden chains, enter his confessional with twisted faces and come out as bright as angels. Why not himself whose burden of sin was so hard to bear?

Then he thought of Teccosi, of Leone, of the good pay, of the cold, damp cell in the half-ruined cloister in the Apennines to which he would have to return, of the shame he would have to acknowledge on his knees before his brother monks in the chapter. The brief good impulse was stifled.

"Mind your own business", he said tartly. Yet he knew that he was on the defensive. Philip's patience and meekness had almost brought him to his knees.

Leone too was weakening. But, unlike Arminio,

Leone did not admit, or even recognize, that Philip's kindnesses—indeed, his constant prayers and penances—were wearing down his contempt and pride. He felt an increasing irritation with this impossibly virtuous man. Yet Leone was drawn to Philip like an iron filing to a magnet. He could not let him alone. The more Philip loved him, the more Leone thought he hated Philip.

Philip fell ill. The doctors, alarmed at the rapid, heavy beating of his heart and the fever that accompanied it, had recommended bleeding. So Philip was cupped and bled. What little strength he had was sucked away. He no longer drank wine for fear of heating his blood. This too weakened him. For a week he had not been able to say Mass. Strangely Leone missed him. He had no one to abuse. He choked upon his unspent anger.

Then suddenly Philip appeared in the sacristy at midday as the two sacristans were ready to close the church. He was as white as marble, save for the tiny blue veins that streaked his almost transparent skin.

"Good day", he said almost timidly.

Arminio gazed at him in alarm. Never had he seen such holiness in a human face. He felt terror in the presence of Philip's innocence. But Leone acted like a rabid dog. He swore foully.

"You little white plaster saint, why didn't you die as your friends said you would? Why didn't you go to heaven? You're a filthy hypocrite. I'll bet you had a fine time entertaining your fancy friends, lying in bed while honest men were working."

Philip's gaze fell to the floor. At that moment the sun burst through the sacristy window and touched the edge of Philip's biretta. To Arminio it was a sign. He knew Philip was a saint. He could bear it no longer.

"Stop it, Leone. This man has done no evil. He never did. It is we who are evil."

Leone's brutish eyes glowered. "He's a liar, a swindler, a cheat, a cad. Look, he can't even defend himself. Watch, I'll spit in his face and he won't dare deny my words." Leone stepped towards Philip as if to make good his threat.

It was too much for Arminio. "He's a good man, I say, a good man."

In a flash he was at Leone's side. His hands reached for Leone's thick neck. His fingers pressed the soft muscles of his throat. He jerked his knee into Leone's soft, swollen stomach. They fell together on the floor, Leone grunting and gasping, Arminio screaming hysterically.

Philip grabbed Arminio's shoulders and heaved him to his feet. Slowly he helped Leone arise. The two men, panting like spent animals, stood a few feet apart, but still locked in hate. Gradually the flames of wrath died out of their eyes and there crept in shame and disgust.

Philip went first to Arminio, whispering, "Forgive him as I forgive you. God give thee peace." Then he turned to Leone, who pushed him away before he could speak. Arminio was now weeping silently. He looked wonderingly at his hands, as if they actually were red with blood. He hung his head. Turning away, he slunk out of the room.

Leone's hairy fingers fondled the purplish red welts on his neck. His eyes looked stunned and surly. His thick underlip quivered resentfully. Finally he, too, left the sacristy.

That day Philip's Mass was one of reparation. Alone in the church he wept and pleaded with God. "Only you can touch their hearts, only you can make them see."

During his thanksgiving he promised a thousand prayers—the Forty Hours devotion, a pilgrimage to the seven churches, a visit to the catacombs, all the penances he could perform—all this for his enemies, particularly for Vincenzo Teccosi, for Arminio, and for Leone. He stormed heaven and won.

First Arminio met him at the door of the sacristy one morning and said, "Leone and I are reconciled."

Philip praised him with a joyous smile.

Then Arminio said hesitantly, stuttering, "May I serve your Mass?"

Philip embraced him. "Of course. Would that I could serve yours."

Shortly afterwards Arminio made his confession to Philip and returned to his order.

Within a week Leone was on his knees, sobbing

his remorse. After he confessed his sins and received absolution, he kissed Philip's hand and wet it with his tears.

"Remember, dear Father Philip, some day you will meet another sinner. If you have trouble converting him, as you did me, remember that there will be a store of prayers waiting for you to use as you will. They will be mine, dear Father. I shall pray for your intention every day of my life."

The doctor was shaken by the conversion of his two sacristans. He began to feel that no man, save a saint of God, could meet constant hostility with such serenity and meekness. He could even sense Philip's prayers working on his own soul. Try as he would, he could no longer resent Philip's piety or the devotion of his followers.

When he went into San Girolamo now and saw the lines stretching in front of Philip's confessional, he was forced to admit that Philip had brought nothing but good to Rome. The confraternity too had gained rather than lost by Philip's presence. Never before had he known such generous response to the needs of the poor, such widespread love of the Blessed Sacrament.

He came to see that Philip was not a revolutionary but a restorer. He was another Saint Benedict, another Saint Francis of Assisi calling the people back to the old Christian way of life.

Vincenzo Teccosi was not one to do things half

way. He was a good hater and a good lover. When he was wrong he was very wrong and when he was right he was very right. He wanted to make it up to Philip.

"There'll be no sneaking up to the back door with a 'Father, I'm sorry'. None of that", he promised himself. So he waited until Philip was preaching one day in a room at the side of the church. As usual, a great crowd was listening. Vincenzo had to jostle his way up to the speaker's desk. He stared at Philip, trying to catch his eye. But Philip, fearing that the physician had come to mock him, avoided his gaze. Vincenzo coughed, as if demanding attention. Still Philip did not recognize him.

At last came the time when Philip allowed his audience to ask him questions. As soon as Philip said, "And now, who wishes to speak?" Ser Vincenzo stepped forward. "I, Vincenzo Teccosi, wish to speak."

In their friendship for Philip the congregation stirred angrily and murmured. Teccosi held up his hand.

"I wish to say to you, Father Filippo, and to all who hear me, that I have persecuted you in thought, word, and deed most unjustly. I am sorry for this with all my heart. I kneel before your reverence and beg your pardon. From this day until the day I die I shall be among your most loyal followers."

So saying he knelt down before Philip and kissed

his hand. Cries of amazement rose from all over the room. Philip bent down and, lifting up his former enemy, embraced him with tears of joy.

"Vincenzo," he cried, "Vincenzo, my brother, what great things we will do for God now that we are united."

From then until the day of his death Vincenzo Teccosi never missed his daily visit to his friend and spiritual father, Philip Neri.

11

PHILIP FOUNDS THE ORATORY

After two years of persecution Philip, by God's grace, had won over the authorities at San Girolamo. Those who were once his enemies were now his dear friends, even his devoted followers. To make the victory still more complete, the cardinal protector of the confraternity decided to appoint a superior of San Girolamo to prevent such abuses in the future. And the superior he selected was none other than Buonsignore Cacciaguerra.

This holy priest, who had suffered as keenly as Philip, lost no time in repairing the damage of two years' scandal. No sooner was he named superior than he called Philip to his room. Philip suspected he would hear good news, but he was hardly prepared for so much of it.

"My authority has been clearly defined", Cacciaguerra said. "The cardinal has given me the right to appoint and dismiss the chaplains of the confraternity and the other priests in the house. I am in charge of the church."

He picked up a letter and waved it in the air. "When I received this letter my first thought was of you, Philip. Now I give you permission to bring your friends here. It is you, Philip, who must be the heart of San Girolamo. For, to tell the truth, dearest friend, I am old and weary. Henceforth my way is the way of prayer and meditation."

Humility, joy, confidence, gratitude—all these streams mingled in one river of love. He thanked Cacciaguerra. He spent many, many hours that day before the Blessed Sacrament, many hours that night on the loggia above San Girolamo where he continued to walk with his all-merciful Lord.

The heart of San Girolamo—yes, Philip was exactly that. Disciples streamed to him to warm themselves in the fire of his love and in the sunshine of his joy. It was Philip who inspired an ever increasing devotion. But he was the head as well as the heart of the reform of Christian Rome.

Philip always claimed he was an ignorant man. "All that I ever knew about prayer I learned as a boy from the Dominicans at San Marco, or as a young man from Ignatius and the Jesuits", he said when his disciples praised him.

Yet, in the most natural, unassuming way Philip founded a school of Christian perfection. He received permission from Cacciaguerra to build a room above the aisle of San Girolamo, which he called the oratory. There he gathered together a brilliant group of men. Some were secretaries at the papal court, others were poets, musicians, and university students. They met in the afternoons to read and discuss the Gospels, the lives of the saints, the history of the Church. At the end of each discussion the musicians in the group led the company in singing. For Philip music was always a way to refresh men's souls and to lift up their hearts to God.

There were evening meetings too, but these were of a different character. These began with a half-hour of mental prayer, after which came litanies, the adoration of the cross, and the recitation of the psalms and prayers to our Lady.

Thus, in the meetings at the oratory, as well as by private conversations in his little room at San Girolamo, Philip was teaching men to mortify themselves and live better Christian lives.

Week after week, year after year the work went on. Here Philip trained priests who later became the bishops and cardinals who were to lead the

Church through difficult times. Here, too, were formed laymen and laywomen whose pious lives gradually spread the Christian leaven throughout Rome.

Some of Philip's disciples remained with him, became priests, and formed the core of a new Christian family, the Congregation of the Oratory.

But the oratory not only drew men to itself; it also gave itself to men. Even those who shunned it—the fickle, the weak, and the wicked—could not but know of its existence. For Philip continued to send his disciples to the hospitals and orphanages, to the slums and byways. The fire he kindled in the breasts of priests, clerics, and laymen flamed out in sermons, in almsgiving, and in works of mercy. Then, too, there were the great public activities of the oratory—the pilgrimages.

At first Philip used to make the pilgrimage to the seven churches alone. He would walk to St. Peter's and pray at the tomb of the first Pope. From there he would go to St. Paul's and pray again. To him this combination of prayer and exercise refreshed both soul and body. He would go then along the Way of the Seven Churches to his favorite church of San Sebastiano, where he would pray in the catacombs. The road led from there to the Lateran, thence to Santa Croce and San Lorenzo, and finally to Santa Maria Maggiore. The whole pilgrimage was twelve miles in length. It took the better part of a day.

As the oratory developed, however, Philip could not, even if he so desired, make this pilgrimage alone. His penitents and followers would not allow so long an absence, so he took them with him. Word spread quickly. The Dominican master of novices heard of it. What more wonderful way was there to have his young charges meet, know, and perhaps even imitate this saintly friend of his order?

"Go, then, all of you", he said to his young novices. "Listen to the reverend father's words. Tell me all he said when you return. Perhaps he will linger awhile at St. Onofrio's on the way back and play a game of quoits or tennis with you."

"But will we not distract him from his prayers?" a timid novice asked.

"No, never fear that you will annoy him. He loves the young. He will cherish your spiritual childhood."

To a serious novice he said, "Of course you may ask him questions. Go to confession to him if you like. You may talk as much as you like. He has said again and again that he would let young men chop wood on his back if that would keep them from idleness, vanity, or sin."

The Capuchins heard of it and, since many of their leaders had consulted with Father Philip on religious matters, they, too, wanted to participate. Eventually the pilgrimages numbered as many as 2,000 at a time.

The pilgrims formed separate bands, some singing on the way, some reciting the Rosary, some chanting the psalms. Philip hopped back and forth, greeting his many friends. "Is there not more joy in this than in the carnival?" For Philip had at last found in the pilgrimage to the seven churches his answer to the carnival.

When they reached San Sebastiano, usually near noon, Mass was said, and, after Mass, the whole throng moved on to the estate of one of Philip's friends, where they ate heartily and rested. Then the hymns started again and on they went, seeking out Christ in his sacramental presence as the ancient Jewish throng followed him when he preached on the shores of Galilee.

In these pilgrimages worldliness met an unanswerable challenge. For here was true joy, joy that would last forever, an ardor that put to shame the carnival revelry that ended in wasteful self-indulgence and in so many violent deaths.

Yet even now, when Philip was already honored as the second apostle of Rome, he still had his enemies. Nor were they all merely spiteful men. No—many of his new enemies were stern men who were frightened by the spread of heresy.

Here is the way they thought. Luther and the other reformers had made changes in the Church's procedures. Philip, too, is making changes. He is encouraging frequent, even daily, confession and

Communion. He is staging unusual religious exercises in the oratory, where laymen as well as priests read and discuss sacred Scripture and musicians give concerts. He is stirring up the public by his pilgrimages and winning a vast personal following. In addition, he has won the friendship of noble families, many of whom venerate him as a saint. He dances and sings, and has his young priests read joke books to him in the presence of important people.

In 1559 these impressions reached the suspicious ears of Virginio Rosario, the cardinal vicar of Rome, the man whose authority in Rome was second to that of the Pope himself. The cardinal either did not know, or forgot, or chose to ignore, Philip's record of fidelity to Christian doctrine, of his prudence in guiding the oratory. He summoned Philip and angrily, contemptuously, he condemned him.

"Your reverence is in danger of prison. I forbid you to go about the city. I forbid you to hear confessions for a fortnight. I forbid all exercises of the oratory unless you receive special permission. Finally, I demand from you the promise to appear before a tribunal such as I see fit to appoint and to answer such charges as may be presented against you."

Of course Philip was stunned. Any false accusation is bitter. Bitterest of all are accusations delivered by one's lawful superior. Moreover, whatever his personal faults, the cardinal was Philip's true lord.

Philip never questioned his authority. He bowed his head and said, "I will obey, my lord cardinal."

But obedience did not satisfy the cardinal. He expected an expression of shame, if not a confession of guilt. Philip's attitude was quite the contrary. Small, meek, courteous he was, but he was calm, too, and clearly ready to defend himself. The cardinal resented Philip's composure.

"I am surprised you are not ashamed of yourself", the cardinal said. "You, who pretend to despise the world, go about enticing numbers of people to follow you. It is to win favor with the multitude and to work your way into some high position while pretending to be so holy."

The words cut Philip worse than the iron chains he wore as a penance. He bit his lips. Silence was his favorite reply to calumny. Yet silence here might be a confession of guilt. Thus silence might be a lie. So he spoke in his usual sweet, low voice:

"My lord cardinal, I began these exercises for the glory of God. For the glory of God I am ready to give them up. I regard my superior's commands as above all other things, and I gladly obey them now. I began the visits to the seven churches as recreation for my penitents and to withdraw them from those occasions of sin which abound during the carnival. This was my purpose and no other."

If ever there was an answer soft enough to turn away wrath, it was this straightforward, respectful reply of Philip. But it only enraged the cardinal.

"You are an ambitious fellow. You are not doing all this for the glory of God but to get together a sect."

The charge of heresy brought a quick blush of dread to Philip's cheeks. Philip raised his eyes to the crucifix. "Lord, thou knowest my mind and heart." He bowed and left the cardinal's presence.

What an agony it was to await that trial! When his followers assembled for the usual exercises, he had to tell them to go away quietly. But, of course, this did not satisfy them at all.

"Why? Why, Father Philip?" they continued to ask.

They refused to believe that he was accused of teaching false doctrines and of acting from unworthy motives. What? Philip a heretic? Preposterous. Ambitious for a bishopric? This was contrary to all their convictions. They would have a thing or two to say to Cardinal This and Bishop That. No processions either? Well, then, they would follow Philip as he walked down the street—at a distance, though. If they remained within earshot Philip would scold them. In all this trouble his deepest concern was not for his own reputation but for that of his enemies. He feared, and rightly, that his friends would think ill of the cardinal and Philip's other accusers. By thinking ill, they would break the Christian unity and peace that Philip was so anxious to restore to Rome.

Did they not know that the answer to all our

problems was acceptance of God's will, no matter how hard that acceptance seemed to be? God's will be done. His Kingdom come. Endure and pray. These were his watchwords.

To his intimate disciples Philip said, "This is not your worry. This persecution is not for your sake but for mine. God desires to make me humble and patient. When I have gathered from this trial the fruit he wills me to gather, it will pass away. Do not console me by arguments. Pray. Pray. Pray."

Still the prospect of the trial hung over the group at San Girolamo. They prayed and they hoped. Rumor reached them that an ecclesiastical commission had been appointed and that the cardinal himself would be a member of it. Rumor had it, too, that the mere accusations against Philip had already turned the weak-minded against him. "Did you hear. . . ? isn't it shocking. . . ? I always knew he was crazy . . . he should be locked up in a monastery . . . he lacks the gravity of a true religious. . . ." These and a thousand other statements were reported to the priests of San Girolamo. Philip continued to pray.

It was now close to the end of the fortnight's suspension. Would the ban against the oratory be lifted or reimposed? When would the summons to the trial come? Philip was in the oratory praying. At his side were his close friends, Francesco Tarugi among them. Suddenly, out of nowhere, a strange priest burst in. The visitor wore a coarse robe bound with a cord. He had an unearthly look about him. He had a message, he said. Certain religious, whom he did not name, had received a revelation. The Oratorians were not to worry. Instead they should begin the Forty Hours devotion. Great blessings would flow from it.

They could believe neither their eyes nor ears. Who was this strange man? Before they could inquire, the visitor turned to Tarugi. Speaking in tones of great gravity he said to him, "This persecution will soon end in the establishment and increase of the work. God will change the hearts of those who are now opposing it so that they will become its supporters. Those who persist in attacking it will be severely punished by God. The prelate who has been foremost and most unjust in the persecution will die in a fortnight." Then the visitor disappeared.

Who this visitor was they never knew. But certainly his message was prophetic. They celebrated the Forty Hours devotion with simple confidence. Soon afterward Philip appeared before his judges. One by one the vague charges against him disappeared before his radiant innocence. As he answered questions his judges became more his disciples than his examiners. They restored to him permission to hear confessions, to teach, to visit the seven churches. Even more, they advised him to do whatever he thought best for the glory of God and the good of souls. All praised him save one man, Virginio Rosario, the cardinal vicar of Rome.

Within fifteen days, as the mysterious visitor had predicted, the cardinal was stricken in the palace of the Pope. He died almost immediately.

One of Philip's staunchest supporters cried out, "Now we can see whether this work was from God. Let him who opposes us take heed of the end that awaits him!"

But Philip did not celebrate his acquittal. He quieted the turbulent joy of his followers. God was good. It was ill payment to his divine providence to rejoice in the death of one's enemies. Philip said, "Pray hard for the cardinal, for he was the instrument, whether he knew it or not, of God's mercy."

Modestly Philip thanked the Pope, Paul IV, for the two candles he sent as a token of good will. Modestly he watched his oratory grow in influence—as the mysterious visitor had prophesied.

The future of his work was now assured. Philip would continue to suffer the usual trials of a reformer and founder of a congregation—misunderstandings, false charges, flash-in-the-pan vocations, ceaseless demands that he do this and that rather than what he knew God intended him to do. But, in general, his work would move forward with uninterrupted success.

12

"GIVE ME MY LOVE QUICKLY"

IN 1595 PHILIP NERI was eighty years old. He was now feeble, shriveled, ailing. His face was as white as his beard; his frame was bent; he tottered when he walked. He needed Father Antonio Gallonio, who slept in the room below his at Vallicella, to help him dress and get about. One cough in the middle of the night was enough to rouse Father Antonio. At the second cough the young priest was already thudding up the stairs.

"What is it, reverend Father? Do you need the doctor, a drink of water? Come, let me prop you up."

Dear, devoted Antonio, the latest of his many sons—some of them already in heaven with Persiano Rosa, some now administering the oratory in his stead, some directing the offices and congregations of the Roman Curia. Philip had lived to become an intimate of popes and cardinals, the spiritual father of hundreds of priests and religious, the confessor and director of countless men and women of the world.

He was really overwhelmed with honors. Pope Gregory XIII had been his intimate friend; Sixtus V admired him. Gregory XIV, now gloriously reigning, regarded him as a brother. When Philip had knelt to perform his homage to the new Pope, Gregory had lifted him up, embraced him, and placed his own cardinal's biretta on Philip's head. "We create you cardinal", he said.

"No, no, no", Philip whispered in his ear. "Let us pretend you were joking."

The Pope gave in to Philip, but he favored him still, never permitting him to kneel or stand in his presence, readily permitting him to say Mass privately in a little chapel next to his bedroom. Philip no longer needed to restrain his ecstasies for fear of scandalizing the timid.

The Sacred College of Cardinals honored him, too. Not a day passed but that Cardinal Borromeo, or Cardinal Cusano, or the Cardinals Paleotto and Valiero, did not come to his room to discuss with him matters that lay on their consciences.

He received all of those who came to see him—old friends, sons and grandsons of former penitents, country cousins of men and women whom he had cured of sickness or of sin. Indeed, he was often vexed with his dear son, Germanico Fedeli, his secretary, and Antonio Gallonio, his faithful watchdog, because sometimes they tried to spare him. "No, let all come who wish to see me."

Honors! Honors! The more Philip hid himself, the more he was talked about. The great cardinals reported his words in their letters and conversations. Young men treasured his every counsel and quoted him to their friends. Philip himself wrote little. He was sparing even with his letters. But he could not prevent others from writing about him.

Gabriele Paleotto, the cardinal archbishop of Bologna, just that year had written a treatise, *The Blessedness of Old Age*. This book was really about Philip himself. Although it proposed to set before the reader in a general way the dignity and majesty of long service to God, the model was plainly Philip. There were many instances of elderly saints, but Cardinal Paleotto could think of but one outstanding example.

"Not only has he spent his days so as to gain the praise of all, but he has in a most wonderful manner stirred up and aided others to live holy and religious lives. Him, therefore, I set before you as a living example of what old age may be; and he is Father Philip Neri of Florence, now in the eightieth year of his age, and who, like a time-honored tree, has for so long a time reached forth to the people the abundant fruit of his virtues. . . . Philip so resolutely despises all earthly good that, although esteemed and beloved by popes and cardinals, he seeks no other dignity and honor than those which are eternal."

And only a few years before, Agostino Valiero, cardinal bishop of Verona, had published a dialogue entitled, "Philip, or Christian Cheerfulness", that set forth in flowing language Philip's own doctrine of boundless charity.

One day Philip said to the cardinal, "I have just now read your book. Ah, Agostino, my son, little did I know that you were taking notes on our conversations."

His fingers clutched a button on Valiero's robe, twisting it as he did habitually when he talked. "It is an exaggeration. But, since you wrote it in the spirit of love, I will forgive you."

Pop. The button came off. Philip seized the second button, looking into Valiero's smiling eyes. "Not only have you made *me* say things more eloquently than I know how to, but your dialogue awards a splendid style to the lord Cardinals Cusano and Borromeo and to the others. You give us an air of culture . . ."

Pop. The second button came off. "I shall soon have you unfrocked, my son." Cardinal Valiero laughed.

"But you have called me a bad name—a Christian Socrates. Such nonsense! And you have made me out to be clever! Really, now, do I ever say one thing that is original or clever? I tell you that joy consists in resigning ourselves wholly and forever into God's hands. I warn you against setting your heart on riches, or power. I tell you to meditate on death, to spend your time with learned and holy men, to use the sacraments, to do good to all around us, to pray without ceasing. Has not all this been said before, and better, by the Master himself, by the Fathers and Doctors of the Church? Agostino, I am an echo, that is all."

Agostino, gazing fondly at his spiritual father, heard the last button of his robe pop.

"Not an echo, Father Philip, but a voice", he said. Philip did seem to be a voice of Christ himself. He lived intimately with the original Source of all life, all truth. His oneness with Christ was his secret, his sweetness, his force, his perpetual fountain of love and cheerfulness. His Christlike charm, impossible to describe, won all hearts. It was the charm of a window, beautiful in itself, but more beautiful because it looked out to the indescribable beauty of Christ.

That was what drew men to Philip. That was why heretics on the way to the stake and Jews confined to the ghetto of age-old fears and prejudices yielded to Philip's persuasion while they resisted to the death the force and argument of other men. That was why all Rome now honored Philip.

But if the last years of Philip's life were full of honors and peace and Christian blessedness, they were not without suffering. Many times Philip had been ill; several times he was anointed and given up for dead. He ate little, slept briefly, disciplined himself continually.

Once, a year before his death, his pulse almost disappeared after twenty-five days of suffering. He was, to all appearances, dying. The curtains on his bed were drawn. The doctors, Angelo da Bagnorea and Ridolpho Silvestri, and the priests of Vallicella waited in the corner, silent with anguish.

Suddenly, from behind the curtains, they heard Philip cry out in a loud firm voice. "He who desires aught else but God is miserably deceived. Ah, my most holy Madonna, my beautiful Madonna, my blessed Madonna!"

They rushed to the bed. There was Philip, his face radiant, his arms outstretched, weeping and calling upon our Lady. Most amazing of all, his body was raised in the air. He seemed to be embracing someone with such affection that he trembled all over, and the very room seemed to shudder.

The startled physicians and their companions heard him say, "No, no, I am not worthy! Who am I, O my dear Madonna, that thou shouldst come to see me? O Virgin most beautiful and most pure, I do not deserve a grace so great. Ah, why art thou come to me, the least and lowest of thy servants?"

For some minutes he went on weeping and talking. Although those about the bed knew of Philip's ecstasies and visions, they were nevertheless astonished by the sight they were witnessing. Should they withdraw? No, duty compelled them to remain. The physicians consulted with each other. They decided to interrupt him.

"Father Philip, what is the matter? We see nothing. Whom do you embrace? With whom are you talking?"

Instantly Philip sank upon the bed. "Then did you not see the Mother of God come to visit me and to take away all my pains?"

When Philip spoke these words he came to himself and looked about him. Then, realizing that he had unwittingly revealed the gift of God's grace to so many people, he began to weep. Instinctively he pulled the sheet over his head. So violent was his weeping that the doctors again feared that he might exhaust his feeble strength.

"Stop, Father Philip, stop at once", Bagnorea said. At length, the sobbing ceased. Silvestri gently pulled away the sheet. Philip's face was serene, his eyes bright and joyous. He smiled at the two physicians.

"I do not need you any longer now; the most holy Mother has come to me and cured me."

Instinctively Bagnorea reached for Philip's wrist. The pulse was steady and firm. He felt Philip's head. The fever had gone. Bagnorea motioned to Silvestri, who repeated his colleague's gestures.

"He *is* well again", Silvestri said. "Our Lady has cured him."

Hearing this, Philip reached out and grasped Bagnorea's arm. "Dear friend, not a word of this to a soul." He raised his voice a little. "All of you—I beg you—repeat nothing of what I may have said."

But it is rarely given to men to witness a miracle. Being a physician, Angelo da Bagnorea felt it was his duty to give a clear account of the event. The priests could not resist the ardent entreaties of Cardinals Cusano and Borromeo. The Pope heard of it. Philip's recovery stirred endless questions. Finally Philip gave in and told what had occurred.

"Be sure of this, my sons", he kept repeating from this time until his death. "Believe me, for I know it well, there is no more effectual means of obtaining graces from God than the most holy Madonna. This very evening say to her, 'Virgin Mother of God, pray to Jesus for me.'"

A year later, another miracle seemed to occur. On the twelfth of May Philip suddenly became worse. His pulse faltered. Cesare Baronius, now head of the Congregation of the Oratory, was summoned. He anointed the unconscious Philip. In a little while the patient's strength revived. Cardinal Borromeo, who had arrived meanwhile, quickly noticed this. He went to the chapel and withdrew the Viaticum. When he brought the Blessed Sacrament into the room Philip burst into tears. With an energy incredible in one so weak he called out, "Behold my Love! Behold my Love! Behold my Love! Behold my only God. Give me my Love quickly, quickly."

He repeated the *Domine, non sum dignus* firmly and devoutly.

"O my Lord, I am not worthy of thee, and I never have been worthy of thee. I have never done one single good thing."

When he received Holy Communion he said, "Now I have received the true Physician of my soul. He who seeks aught but Christ knows not what he seeks."

During the remainder of that day he suffered greatly. A great smothering pain tore at his chest. He coughed and spat blood. It seemed that he could not possibly survive the night. Yet the next morning he greeted his physicians cheerfully.

"Be off with you all", he said, "I've had Masses said and sent alms to the convents and I'm better. I've no pain. Here, feel my pulse."

They examined him carefully. It was as he said. He was cured. He got out of bed at once and resumed his daily tasks. He said Mass, read his Office, heard confessions. For ten days he was his old self—cheerful, even radiant. But he knew he was going to die, even to the day and the hour.

In 1595 the feast of Corpus Christi—Philip's last day on earth—came on May 25. He spent it exactly as God intended and as he himself wished. He had given word that he would hear confessions early that morning. His penitents came before daybreak. After confessions, he said his Mass, singing the *gloria* exultantly, reciting the prayers with extraordinary fervor. He received his guests with more affection than usual. Angelo da Bagnorea dropped in for a friendly chat. Casually he felt Philip's wrist.

"You are better now than you ever have been. I haven't seen you in such good health in ten years."

Philip smiled at him. These doctors—how much they knew, how little they knew. Bagnorea did not know God's will in this matter. Cardinal Cusano stopped by three times, the last time to make his confession. Philip accompanied the cardinal as far as the stairs, pressed his hands warmly, and looked at him long and lovingly. He heard more confessions until ten o'clock.

As he prepared himself for bed, Gallonia heard him say, "Well, last of all, one has to die. Three and two are five, three and three are six, and then we shall go. Now, then, Antonio, go and take your rest."

At the sixth hour of the night Gallonio heard Philip walking in the room above. He awoke, as he had so many times before, and ran to Philip's room. Philip was sitting at the side of his bed, choking and spitting.

"How do you feel, Father Philip?" Antonio said automatically.

"I am dying, Antonio."

Gallonio sent for the doctors. He woke up Baronius and the other fathers. They crowded into the room, knelt down, and began the prayers for the dying. The physicians came. This time they were certain. Philip was dying. His eyes were closed. He was barely breathing.

Baronius spoke out. "Father, Father, are you leaving us without a word?"

The eyelids flickered. "If you cannot speak, give us at least your blessing", Baronius begged.

Philip opened his eyes. First he looked upward, then he fixed his gaze on his sons. He moved his hand in a faint movement of blessing. Then he sighed deeply and fell asleep in Christ.

After his death the doctors who had been attending him opened the body to examine the great swollen heart. They found that the heart was unusually large, the pulmonary artery twice the normal size. Two of the ribs over the heart were broken and arched outward. As they suspected, there was no sign of disease. They were convinced that the enlargement of the heart was a sign of divine possession.

Rome mourned the death of its second apostle.

Its citizens built for him a rich and beautiful tomb. Soon they rejoiced in the miracles obtained by the use of his relics, by the prayers of intercession that streamed to him. Two months after his death the process of beatification began. In 1615 Pope Paul V declared him blessed. Finally Rome rejoiced when Pope Gregory XV declared Philip a saint on March 12, 1622. Canonized with him were two dear friends, Ignatius of Loyola and Francis Xavier, and two others very much after his own mind, Isadore, the simple farmer of Madrid, and Teresa of Avila, she of the flaming heart.